Starts out pretty good but gets drawn out

+5

A boy meets girl book

CANDLELIGHT REGENCY SPECIAL

CANDLELIGHT REGENCIES

MAKESHIFT MISTRESS

Amanda Mack

A CANDLELIGHT REGENCY SPECIAL

Published by
Dell Publishing Co., Inc.
1 Dag Hammarskjold Plaza
New York, New York 10017

Dell ® TM 681510, Dell Publishing Co., Inc.

ISBN: 0-440-15874-5

Printed in the United States of America

First printing—January 1981

Chapter One

The late January day had been mild and pleasant until four in the afternoon when the wind changed and came out of the northeast, thrusting black snow clouds into the Leicestershire sky. The storm wind swooped across the rolling countryside, lashing the spinneys and bending the trees in the hedgerows. It took no second sight to know the thaw was over. The birds roosted early in the innermost thickets; the small animals took refuge in their holes. The only living creature remaining on the land was a woman carefully picking her way through the rutted lane, her attention fixed on the driest course between the mudholes. She was unaware of the weather change until her black woolen cloak was caught and whirled wildly around her. Before she could react, the wind wrenched off her bonnet, her pearl-headed hatpin notwithstanding, and flung it willy-nilly into a neighboring field. The once neatly bound long blond hair whipped about her face as she turned to watch the bonnet collapse into a brush pile. There could be no thought of retrieving it. Her boots were made for town pavements, not country roads, and had already proven inadequate.

Elizabeth's only regrets were for the loss of a bonnet scarcely two months old. She was too tired after almost twenty-three hours of traveling to care about her disheveled appearance. To rally her spirits, she tried to concentrate on her destination—the house which the innkeeper vowed was a scant seven miles down this road—but her mind kept straying. Why had she not waited sensibly in the comfort of the inn until morning? By then the wheel would be repaired and she could have hired the horse and trap. But half an hour ago it had seemed pigeonhearted to stop this close—and the innkeeper had assured her it was an easy walk. The only wise thing she had done was to leave her bag at the inn, and that was not because it would have been hard to manage, but because she was unsure of her reception. Oh, for the days when she was young, happy, and in good health! The whole journey from Margate would have been nothing. The walk would have been polished off in no time and the evening spent dancing!

All that was before Cuidad Rodrigo and Ian's death, a long two years ago. Now at twenty-eight Elizabeth finally had learned to be a widow. It had been difficult. There had been so little time to be a wife. She tried to dispel her memories, but images of the hospital in Spain filled her. After Ian was killed, she had thrown herself into helping with the sick and wounded. To the men and their overworked surgeons, she had been a godsend—a woman unafraid of horrors. No one understood she was dead inside, as dead as her husband in his rock-covered grave. How could their charnel house hold any fear for her? When typhus swept through the hospital, Elizabeth worked even harder, until she too fell sick. At last she had hope; soon she would rejoin her husband. Instead she lived; but the baby, the baby she had not known she was carrying—Ian's child—died.

Elizabeth could not permit her mind to continue; there must be no more self-pity. But the view of the bleak hills under the black sky encouraged melancholy and, to fight this Stygian darkness, she made herself think of Margate. They had sent her to that charming seaside resort to convalesce. Her recovery had taken almost two full years, for neither her mind nor her body had wished to be well. *Facilis est descensus Averni,* one of her father's favorite lines, now held special meaning for her. At last, however, the bracing Channel air, the motherly care of her landlady, Mrs. Parrott, and time itself all had their effect. The benumbed, wraithlike creature who had been carried into her lodgings was a whole woman again.

Her doctors told her she was ready to take command of her own life once more. The autocratic Dr. Forrester was uncompromising in his pronouncement. "Twenty-eight is not old, Mrs. Campbell. You're a handsome woman—there's still plenty of life ahead of you. Get yourself married again, or do good works, but you *must* do something!"

Elizabeth knew they were right, but she would never remarry. She had no need or desire for another man—ever. Yes, there was a life before her. It would be without Ian, and now that she was calmer, she could think of him without the pain filling her. No, there would be no more regrets for marrying the soldier, and if the heights of life were over for her, so would she escape the valleys of despair. Calmly and rationally her life would be planned. In the future she must never allow herself to become as exhausted as she was now, for then doubts and self-pity crept in.

At the top of a rise Elizabeth paused to catch her breath and rub her icy hands, for whether she tried to keep the hood on or the cloak around her, her hands were exposed. Thin town gloves, though woolen, were of no use against the penetrating cold. Bother all shire winds! And their so-called roads too! Her father's wisdom was reconfirmed; what good sense to drop the connection with this branch of the family. People who willingly lived in such godforsaken places should be forgotten! Elizabeth laughed. She was standing in the middle of the wilds only because of these very cousins. The flapping of her cape brought her back to the present and to the vulnerability of her position, but despite her intentions, her feet refused to move. They were no longer cold or numb; it was as if they were not part of her. Only by pretending that she was in some civilized part of England following a pretty path edged by wild flowers would her feet grudgingly start shuffling down the hill.

Her wretched physical state must be ignored if she was to continue this insane journey. How in heaven's name had she allowed herself to become engaged in such an errand? To be rushing to a cousin whom she had met only once in her life, a girl whose existence was unknown to her six months ago—was this the new, rational Elizabeth?

She had been taking her daily walk on the Margate pier when a well-dressed child darted up and stammered out a "C-C-Cousin Elizabeth?" Before Elizabeth could speak, the girl hastily identified herself as Cousin Cecelia. "I know who you are," she continued, speaking so quickly that the sentences ran together, "for Mummy pointed you out to Cousin Clarice yesterday. Your father and Mummy are first cousins twice removed, and I want you to know I approve of your running away to marry your captain, even if the rest of the family does not!" She was out of breath when she finished, but she resolutely faced the older woman as if to prepare herself for the cut to come.

Elizabeth had not been able to snub Cousin Cecelia; there was something very appealing about the young maiden, for she was older than she had first appeared. Nor did Elizabeth speak of her indifference to *that* family's opinion. What Elizabeth did say was

...g out in the world again!

...tion helped her through the confusion of the stage change, and she savored the sights and sounds of the large city. Later, when she became tired of the noise and jiggling of the coach, it was simple to retreat within herself, to reexamine her own goals and plans. Thus the long hours passed, leaving both her mind and body exhausted. Stuffed between a bony Edinburgh physician and the equally thin wife of a Scunthorpe coal-mine owner, she had been unable to sleep.

It had seemed a good omen, one more reason to reach her cousin tonight, when the innkeeper mentioned that Cecelia's parents were away for a few days. She would be able to talk privately with the girl without having to explain her presence to the mother. Later it occurred to her that her cousin might have considered this an opportune time for the elopement.

Coming out of her reverie, Elizabeth looked up the road, hoping to see some outbuildings, but there was nothing in view except for a few trees which were rapidly becoming covered with snow. While she had darkness was so gh ... could see no farther than a few pac... lane seemed to curve, but there was nothing to indicate that people lived nearby or used the road.

Chapter Two

The elegant blue and silver traveling coach belonging to Edward Charles Augustus Frederick Rawling, fourth Duke of Danforth, sixth Earl of Rawling, Baron Rawling of Taversley, etc., came to a stop on the deserted road. In the last of the twilight the postilions hurried to hold their horse's heads while the footmen lit the coach lamps, exterior and interior. The footmen were back at their places, the postilions remounted on their horses, and the coachman starting up again with no more than a five-minute delay. For once the duke was unappreciative of the efficiency of his servants; he was no longer looking forward to the house party. If his calculations were correct, and they were usually extremely accurate, they should arrive within forty-five mintues. He had decided that he would leave the next morning; that he was coming at all was due only to the fondness which he felt for his host, Lord Eversley.

The duke was regarded as a prime catch in the marriage mart, for he not only held an honorable title, but an equally honorable fortune, one that would allow him to play every night at the Prince of Wales's tables, if his Grace so wished. He was a members of White's, Brooks's and Waiter's, but obsessive gambling no longer held an interest for him. He would drop into his clubs and occasionally play, if it amused him, but it was becoming increasingly difficult to find things that were amusing. He enjoyed his estates, hunting, the fair sex, adding to his already considerable art collection, and such, but not to the degree that he had formerly found them enjoyable.

Over the years the comments of scores of unsuccessful matchmaking matrons had given rise to the general belief that he was a cold man. He was well aware of the mode's pronouncement, and if anything he encouraged the belief, for it gave him more freedom to do as he pleased. The problem now was that he did not know what pleased him. Always a very private person, he increasingly retreated to solitary pleasures or to the company of his intimates, six or seven in number. They knew the duke's warm side. They saw the thoughtfulness and kindness of the man, and shared his sense of fun as well. Even so, had it been anyone other than Eversley, his Grace would have sent a note explaining the situation and conveying his sincere regrets.

When Lord Eversley had proposed spending a couple of weeks in his hunting box in the Melton country, this time sporting with lovelies instead of foxes, it seemed a first-rate idea to the duke and the other four friends. "'Twill be the best way," said Lord Chadderfield, "to shake off the excessive family feeling we all get after our respective Christmases. Not that I've anything against family, but sir, enough's enough!" All that the five must do was arrive before dinner with their own companion; everything else would be provided by their host. As the hunting box had a first-rate cellar and Eversley set a good table, it promised to be an enjoyable break before entering into the frenzy of the season.

The duke had been on the verge of asking a delightful little actress whom he had been pursuing for the last few months, when an old friend had re-entered his life. Georgette had come up to town to take a sad farewell of her marquis, who was leaving for a year's appointment in Vienna. After the tearful adieus she was very agreeable to renewing her friendship with Danforth, readily agreeing to be his guest at Eversley's house party—just the thing to brighten up her spirits. After making all the arrangements for the trip to Eversley's, Danforth left to spend Christmas at his family seat. Georgette was to post up to Nottingham where they would meet, and together they would continue north. The duke was so confident all would go according to plan that he sent his valet ahead to transport the multitude of packages containing additions to Georgette's wardrobe. With him had gone the instructions that they be pressed and hanging as a surprise for the pretty lady.

Instead, when the duke had arrived at the White Stag, in place of Georgette's charming person, he was greeted by the rotund landlord, her note of explanation in hand. Regrettably during her sojourn with the marquis, she had adopted the practice of having an eight-year-old page in constant attendance. The duke had always considered child pages bad *ton*; that Georgette had caught measles from the boy was very fitting, but it left him in the lurch. They were expected in a few hours; it was too late to find a substitute. While Danforth had enjoyed the bawdy house when younger, at thirty-six he was far more fastidious in his selection.

Naturally, as head of the family, the duke considered that he had a duty to marry and beget an heir. Fortunately this obligation could be shelved for a few more seasons. He had watched too many of his friends and acquaintances—certain they had known what they were doing—wake up to find themselves shackled to hen-witted women. Women were either charming or they were intelligent. The few times he found the fortunate combination in one person, she was either married or too old.

None of these ruminations would help him now,

however. He would do the decent thing by making his apologies in person, then hie off to town. His fingers played with the long hairs of the lynx carriage robe as his eyes went to the window. Snow was falling, but it was not enough to bother his cattle. The coach started to take a bend in the road when, with a good deal of oaths, the coachman pulled up his horses. The suddenness of the stop flung the duke off his seat, and he righted himself with an oath of his own.

He threw open his carriage door and began to request the cause of the unexpected stop when he saw the dark object on the ground, almost under the near leader's hooves. One of the footmen was down already and running toward it as the other leaped down to assist his master. Danforth waved him away and jumped into the road himself.

As they neared, they could distinguish the object as a woman. The first footman was brushing the snow off her cloak and trying to help her to her feet. There was no blood or other sign of injury; she did not appear hurt, only dazed. Relief made the duke caustic. "I will not comment, madam, on the unsuitability of walking in this weather. I shall only note that a coach and four do make enough noise so that you could have moved to the side of the road!"

His rudeness and lack of concern helped Elizabeth recover her composure more rapidly than a sympathetic manner could have. She shook off the footman's helping hands and raised herself to confront the churl who had spoken. She was still shaken by the narrow escape, but by speaking slowly, she was able to control her voice. "Sir, if you drove as one should in country lanes, instead of rushing along as if you were on the King's Highway, I should not be, at this very moment, sitting upon very cold, wet ground!" Elizabeth was unable to discern his features, but she kept her head erect, ready to chastise him further.

Danforth was unaccustomed to being on the receiving end of a setdown and was about to rectify this when he belatedly recognized that neither the accent nor the language was rustic but genteel. The second footman was returning with one of the lamps, and the duke motioned him to bring it even closer, the better to inspect her. She was evidently a woman of spirit, but her clothes were without pretention. Her face, however, was remarkable: a full, sensuous mouth, Grecian nose, and yes, large blue eyes flashing with emotion. Her cheekbones were high and white. If they were not frostbitten, they were dangerously close to it.

His Grace was not an impulsive man; it was his practice to coldly weigh all of the odds before making a move. Neither was he a particularly charitable person. Though he was liberal in assistance to his dependents and a few others, the words Good Samaritan would not leap into mind when Danforth's name appeared in conversation. As a connoisseur of the gentle sex, accustomed to the company of known beauties, he certainly had encountered blue eyes before. He therefore confounded everyone, himself included, by bending over and picking up the woman. He was almost to the carriage door before the footmen recovered their aplomb and ran ahead to put down the steps. The duke deposited Elizabeth onto the seat, climbed in after her, and shut the door.

Had Elizabeth been able to call for an immediate accounting, Danforth could not have answered. He had reacted instinctively, not as the discriminating patrician. As Elizabeth stared at him, trying to recover her wits enough to protest, he was caught again by her grave blue eyes. He took her hands, intending to reassure her, but they were cold and wet and whatever he might have said was forgotten as he quickly stripped off the gloves and rubbed her hands to restore the feeling. Elizabeth's teeth began to chatter.

His first thought was for her feet, and he was correct; the stiff, frozen leather boots only served to keep the cold within. He unlaced them as fast as he could untangle the mess of ice, mud, and knots, pulled them off, wiped his hands and her feet with his immaculate white linen handkerchief, and began to massage them. Elizabeth wanted to object to his high-handedness and to the pain, but the warmth of the carriage was as numbing as the snow and cold had been. Her body started to shake; she was almost insensible, and the duke shouted to his coachman to drive on.

It was clear that she was half-frozen. Danforth took off his greatcoat to put over her, but her woolen cloak was so heavily saturated with moisture that it had to be removed first. She was incapable of helping, and it took a good ten minutes to get her out of its folds. As he pulled the last of the cloak away, the lynx rug caught his eye. That would be better than his coat, but she was shaking so hard it would not stay on. It became simpler to bring her into his arms and wrap the rug around them both. Elizabeth could not stop shivering, and he held her as close as he could. Gradually, as the warmth of the rug and the heat of his body seeped through her, she stopped trembling and lay quietly pressed against him.

As warmth penetrated into her body, her mind floated as if it had nothing to do with her physical being. Colors and fragments of thoughts drifted in and out of the darkness and when the body and the mind began to reunite, she knew she was dead or in a dream world. It was unimportant which, for it was a delightful place, not frightening at all, a world she would not have imagined but one she could enjoy. Although it had been over two years since she had been held by a man, her body had not forgotten how to respond. Passion that had died in Spain returned in England, and she raised her head, bringing her lips up, inviting his answer. There was no hesitation. His mouth came down onto hers, responding to her need with a violence of his own.

The coach stopped without disturbing them. They were wholly absorbed in their discovery of each other; their kiss was long, her lips yielding and wanting, his demanding and insistent. Her eyes briefly opened and were caught by those of the duke. They burned into hers, and the fire between them leaped higher as her eyes answered, drawing him deeper into her. His mouth left hers and slowly began to caress her face and neck. She lay still in his arms as if asleep, dreamily accepting, her whole body luxuriating at his touch.

A small corner of her mind began to worry her until she could no longer ignore it. The passion was so patently unreal, a joyous illusion; it was to be enjoyed. She had read of travelers lost in the snow, discovered frozen to death after the terrible storm, but with smiles on their faces. If all entered Elysium in this sensuous manner . . . But how did one account for beard stubble? Why would this be part of the fantasy? Elizabeth made her tired eyes open again.

Which faculty could be trusted? Yes, she could feel the slight irritation on her skin—and his breath— and there was a smell of damp wool intermingled with an exciting masculine scent. She found her left hand and dug her thumb into her little finger. It hurt. This was no hallucination! She truly was in the arms of a man, not a shadow! She was alive, awake, her body held by a stranger—freely, wantonly allowing him to make love to her!

All passion dead, Elizabeth used her remaining strength to pull herself out of his arms. She lay against the seat unable to move or think, the little emotion she could feel, one of horror.

Danforth had not understood the reason for her sudden move. All of her color had gone and he assumed that she felt unwell. He noted that the coach had stopped and was relieved to see the Doric columns of Eversley's portico welcoming them. She needed to be inside. She was a very attractive woman, a most responsive woman. Never again would he scoff at those who believed in manna from heaven! He tucked the rug around her and nodded to the waiting footman to open the door. He descended and reached back to take her in his arms again. As he rearranged the rug around her, he spoke softly into her ear. "We shall talk in a short while, I promise. In the meantime, my dear, do trust me and say nothing." Taking her silence for consent, the fourth Duke of Danforth entered the house carrying in his arms what he considered the answer to his immediate problem.

Chapter Three

At the age of thirty-two, Lord Eversley was a favorite of the *ton*. He was known and liked for his good heart as well as for his good bottom, the latter as important to the fashionable world as his wealth. Hostesses loved him for his cheerful nature and for the unfailing kindness which he showered on both aging dowagers and raw, first-season misses. He had no proclivity for the arts, preferring a good dance, a gallop on one of his hunters, or a drink with his friends to an evening spent with the Muses; but if by chance he found himself at a *soirée musicale*, his excellent manners would carry him through. On the whole his taste in clothes was good, with his tailoring done by Weston. The only exceptions were his waistcoats, for he tended to follow the example of the Tulips rather than that of the Beau or Danforth. His lordship did not neglect the fairer sex, but as both he and his indulgent father agreed that he was much too young to settle down, his favors were distributed among the Cyprian set rather than the *bon ton*.

Although the duke was older and a noted collector of paintings and other objects d'art, while Eversley was a true Philistine, they shared enough other interests to make them good friends. It was observed that when the two were together, the Duke of Danforth's notorious reserve was mollified, and as Lady Jersey remarked, "Why, he can even make Danforth seem human!"

Eversley had become concerned about his friend as he watched Danforth's ennui grow. He had tried heretofore foolproof methods of combating boredom—with no success. Unwilling to abandon his friend as hopeless, Eversley had proposed the house party. He had no plan in mind this time, other than his steadfast optimism that something would turn up.

He was crossing the oak-planked hall to go to the drawing room when the duke entered the house with the draped woman in his arms. The assembled servants watched the arrival with suppressed interest, but no such inhibition kept his lordship from showing his curiosity, and he came bounding up to greet his tardy friend.

"Now dash it, Edward! Here we were thinking you were missing out on the start of all the sport. 'Pears that you started before us! That's not . . ."

The duke wished his kindly host to perdition, for he had counted on a quiet, unannounced arrival and straight to his room; there were several items to be settled before he joined the festivities. Now he would have to deal with Eversley before proceeding as planned. He interrupted his friend.

"Devil take you, Richard! When will you learn that the first duty of a host is to provide comfort for one's guests? I've spent the better part of a day on your damnable roads just to honor you with my presence, and here I am, greeted with reproach instead of cheer! Not only must we provide our own companions, but in all probability, our own provisions and drink as well." Eversley lifted his hands to protest, but the duke continued, "Well, then, I see that there is nothing for it but to go to my room to change." He turned to the waiting butler and nodded that he was ready. "I'll be down in a half hour or so," and still holding Elizabeth, he turned to follow the butler up the stairs.

Before he was halfway up, the duke paused to give his host a parting shot. "Do not worry, Richard," he called down. "It will give you time to send out to the village for something!" He continued up, grinning at the sputtering protests. Now that he had successfully postponed making his new friend known to Eversley, he could plan his own introductions.

The butler turned to the left upon reaching the landing. "You have the north bedchamber, as always, your Grace."

As the duke followed, he debated whether to ask for a maid, as dry garments were a necessity, or if it would not be wiser to have a short, private talk first. He knew himself to be a master in the art of seduction, never having bedded an unwilling woman (not that he could imagine this delightfully responsive woman to be unwilling), but if his proposal for their mutual enjoyment took more than a brief conversation, it would be better without either interruptions or spectators.

The butler stopped at the end of the corridor and opened the large door on the left. "If there is anything you require, your Grace, please to ring the bell." The duke nodded and entered. The butler bowed, gave another very respectful "your Grace," and closed the door.

Lord Eversley had redone the house two years before, removing all traces of the heavy Gothic. The north bedchamber had its woodwork, including the wainscoting, painted a delicate sea-foam green. The walls and ceiling were parchment white, with a light molding of a Greek-key design running along the ceiling and compartmenting the walls. It was a large room, so the massive canopied bed with its green and white damask hangings was not overpowering.

The green velvet window curtains were pulled shut and the candles were lit around the walls and in the candelabras, making the room cheerfully bright.

The duke's dressing gown lay on one of the white damask upholstered grandfather chairs in front of the white marble fireplace. Parker, his valet, was rearranging the logs, but he straightened and then bowed as the duke entered.

"Good evening, sir. You had an agreeable journey, I trust. Good evening, madam," bowing to the bundled form. "Benson assures me that the chimneys have been cleaned since our last visit, so perhaps the smoking is due to the incompetent way the fire was laid. I believe that I have remedied the situation." He moved to stand in one of the window bays so that his master could take the benefit of the fire.

"Good evening, Parker," the duke answered as he crossed to the fireplace. "Allow me, my dear," and he lowered Elizabeth into the empty chair and readjusted the robe so that her body would receive the heat from the fire. He brought up the small upholstered footstool for her feet and rubbed them until they felt a trifle warmer. "There, that should do it," he said, giving them a last pat and rising to his feet.

The duke stretched and brought his hands up to his shoulders several times to restore the circulation as he walked over to the waiting valet. "Parker, if you would drop a word to Hoare. I do not care to have the events of this afternoon bandied about." He nodded his dismissal, but another thought came as Parker was at the door. "By the way, that was evidently Benson who showed me up. Please do tell him again that one 'your Grace' is sufficient."

"Yes, sir," the valet answered and left to carry out his orders. Parker, as a correct gentleman's gentleman, had given no indication that his master's entrance with "friend" in arms had been in any way out of the ordinary. However, when her face had been uncovered, and it was not that of the expected guest —he saw the miserable condition of her dress and person, and her stocking feet!—he had become completely impassive.

First he must go to the stables to find the coachman and discover the details of what must have been a most interesting afternoon. He did not consider it proper that others should know more of his master's business than he, but from the little he already had perceived, it would appear to be a rackety affair. Parker sighed. He would make certain that Hoare kept his lip buttoned. He must not forget to again endeavor to teach his lordship's rather inferior caretaker-cum-butler the rudiments of social etiquette. Parker sighed again. He did not foresee an easy fortnight.

Chapter Four

The comfortable chair and the heat of the fire were restoring a semblance of life to Elizabeth. Her feet and hands tingled as the feeling returned, but her last clear memories were of leaving the stage at the inn, and those were intertwined with the changes in London. She was unable to make the effort to sort through the jumble of dream and fact. She had no idea where she was—other than that it was an elegant establishment. Although it was too much of an effort to look around the room, what could be seen bespoke of great wealth.

Could she have been kidnapped? Elizabeth wondered. How absurd! A widow's two hundred per annum wouldn't make a dent here. Not only was the fireplace of matched white marble, but the two simple columns holding the mantel on either side were of marble too. Now . . . there were always stories of . . . discreet bagnios. Even more ridiculous! No trepanning gang could have any connection with this. Through the large convex mirror with the cupid candle fittings above the mantel, Elizabeth could see the reflection of the long mirror on the opposite wall. It was the height of style, or so she had read.

Through a jumble of thoughts and impressions the words of her doctors recommending a change of surroundings came to the fore. She was not too confused to mark that they undoubtedly had Tonbridge Wells, or even London, in mind, not some luxurious chamber in the north. The more she thought on this and of the reaction of the austere Dr. Forrester, could he see her now, the more Elizabeth was diverted from the mystery of the present. The ludicrousness of it all engrossed her. If she did not feel so fragile, she would laugh, for it was truly funny. Her face lost its tight, pained expression as an impish smile began. A slight movement at her side made her turn her head, and Elizabeth found herself smiling at a very handsome man.

After the valet left, the duke had time to consider the woman in front of the fire. It was not a pleasing sight: the long blond hair was matted and tangled; to call the wet, bedraggled gown dowdy was too kind. The contrast between the gloss of the lynx rug and the shabby, begrimed female disgusted him, for the duke was a discriminating man. She no longer appealed to him sensually. Wondering what in God's name had possessed him, as he walked over to her chair, he began to calculate how much he should give to be rid of her.

The woman turned her head and smiled up at him. Her face was enchanting. The hair and gown were entirely forgotten as the duke responded to her glow of delight. Disarmed and fascinated once again, his lips slowly moved down to cover hers.

Elizabeth was as if mesmerized, watching his lips approach. At last she was able to lift her hand to check them, and the kiss that her fingers received made a thrill run through her tired body. Unquestionably nothing good could come of this; it was imperative that she immediately make this clear. "Sir . . . I am not one of your fancy pieces of goods . . ." Unfortunately she was betrayed by her exhaustion, for her voice softly pleaded rather than loudly announced.

Danforth promptly reassured her. "My dear one," he began as he took her hand, "there is no need to place a name, or even to try to justify something as pleasant as we shall have. That it will be mutually enjoyable, we already know. I give you my word, you will not suffer for it." The hand that he held was clammy; there were beads of perspiration on her face. The duke was contrite. "My sweet, I am truly a brute. Forgive me. You do need a change of clothing this moment!" Dropping her hand, he strode over to the bell rope near the bed.

She spoke as he pulled the bell, but her voice was so low that he asked her to repeat it as he returned to her side.

"I have not known a man since my husband was killed. Nor did I wish one."

He noted her use of the past. "My love, then it is more than time you were awakened. To waste such a passionate nature as yours would be a crime." Danforth remembered another detail which had to be settled. "There is one thing we should dispose of, my sweet one. Who is expecting you? Should a note be dispatched or . . ." He waited for her reply.

Elizabeth could only shake her head, but this immediately brought a sharp, throbbing pain that felt as if her head were being sawed off. Her hands flew up to press her head as hard as she could, but the pain continued.

Parker entered. "You rang, sir?"

"Yes. Send me one of the maids directly. And, Parker, do you have the clothes for my friend unpacked?"

"Oh, yes, sir. They have been pressed and are now hanging in the dressing room, as you requested."

"Good. Then just get me a maid."

Parker bowed and left. The duke knelt before Elizabeth, concerned about her obvious distress.

"You may trust me, my dear. All will be well when you are out of your wet things."

Elizabeth made no answer. Her face was flushed and her hands continued to press into her head. He was about to speak when the door opened and a young female entered.

She wore a small mobcap on her head and an equally small apron around her waist. If she were a maid, she was dressed most uncommonly for her station. Her décolletage almost completely revealed her ample breasts and the hem of her skirt ended just above well-turned ankles. At another time and place the duke might have been amused; this evening he was offended.

She dropped a curtsy, and then giggled. The duke rose to his feet. To a man particular in his horses, his women, and his servants, she was an affront. His face reflected his displeasure, and she tossed her head.

"I'm sorry, I'm sure," she said, and as his face did not lighten, she added, "your Grace."

Before Danforth could order the strumpet out, Elizabeth started to shiver, and he was reminded of the immediate problem. There was nothing for it, he decided. Dry clothes were urgent. The jade would have to do.

"Well, don't stand there gaping. Help the lady out of her wet garments! You'll find others in the dressing room. And be quick about it, for she is not feeling well!" He turned back to Elizabeth and lay his hand on her shoulder to reassure her. "In a few moments, my dear." He turned back to the girl and nodded at her to start as he left the room.

I cannot let myself be sick, Elizabeth kept repeating to herself, I must leave. But almost to the rhythm of her reiteration, alternating waves of heat and cold were sweeping over her.

The girl looked Elizabeth over with a practiced eye. "Hounds tooth," she muttered. "These swells have tastes there's no accounting for! Looks more like something no cat o' mine would drag in than a fancy bit for the likes of him!" She walked over to Elizabeth. "Well, we'd better get you out of those rags and changed, or you'll be no use to him a'tall."

She tried to get Elizabeth to stand, but after one incredulous look, Elizabeth refused to have anything to do with her. Insisting, the girl took hold of her to pull her to her feet. An immediate, sharp blow from Elizabeth's free hand made the girl abandon her plans.

"Hey now!" the girl snapped. "No call for putting the mitts on me! Why, don't you just fancy yourself a regular Jezebel!" She became further enraged when Elizabeth turned her head away. "Well then, old trull, you can dress yourself, you can!" and, giving a flounce of her tightly fitting skirt, she strode out of the room.

Parker was waiting in the hall, and in her anger, the girl turned on him. "Now just you see here, laddie," she snarled. "That sort in there don't want nothing to do with help. Find yourself someone what'll take her ladyship's high and mighty!"

Parker's head went up. "I shall deal with you later," he frigidly assured her. He turned his back on the virago and went to consult with his master. In normal circumstances he would have immediately put the harpy in her place and taken care of the whole situation, but these were not normal times. He shook his head and sighed again.

He found the duke in the drawing room, listening to an extremely defensive Lord Eversley, who was trying to explain the choice of servants for the holiday. " 'Pon rep, Edward! As I said before, you know very well—can't bring regular staff here for a bang up like this! My Maureen got the girls. Won't be a squawk from the bunch. No reason to cut up about them," he ended soothingly. "Really a jolly lot." He smiled engagingly and lifted his glass to his friend.

The duke was not mollified. Although he could see Eversley's point, he did not care to expose his new friend to such a "jolly lot." He postponed his further comments, however, when he saw the grave look on his valet's face.

"There is a slight difficulty, sir," Parker said. "If I might have a few words with you."

The duke frowned. "Damn it, Parker." He put his glass down on the octagonal table and stood up. Bowing to his host, he said, "My excuses, Richard," and still frowning, he preceded his man out of the room.

Chapter Five

Parker quickly related what had happened. There was no comment from his master, so he suggested that Mrs. Benson, the housekeeper, be asked for assistance. Danforth was skeptical; he knew her husband and was singularly unimpressed, but when no other solution came to mind, Parker was given leave to find her.

The duke took the stairs slowly, being engrossed in the complications coming from Eversley's simple invitation. He was both irritated that the trollop had not been summarily dismissed and apologetic that his new friend had been subjected to such a person at all. What was even more disturbing to a stickler on form, he still did not know her name. It relieved him somewhat to damn all small page boys again, and he reached his door in a better frame of mind.

Upon entering, he only had time to note that she was asleep in the chair, for Parker and Mrs. Benson arrived on his heels. Mrs. Benson made a curtsy, straightened up, looked him in the eyes, and waited.

She was as unlike her husband as possible. Where Benson was soft and rounding, she was straight and bony. While Benson enjoyed the noise, the confusion, and the questionable carryings-on, his wife was outspoken in her disdain for the heathenish lot that were his lordship's guests. However, as there was nothing she could say that would make her husband leave his position (with the comfortable remuneration it entailed), it was her moral obligation to respect the nuptial vows. Mrs. Benson performed her duties in an exemplary manner but made it known that she would have nothing to do with any guest. She had consented to come to the duke only because Parker, whom she held in great respect, had been less than precise when he requested her aid.

Danforth was in an uncomfortable position. The rank of a housekeeper precluded this sort of thing, and the duke did not care to ask favors, especially of this purse-mouthed woman; however, his friend was still sleeping (pray she was not sick) and at this stage of their friendship it would be wiser to have a female assist. He became very formal as he announced, "Madam is not feeling well. I am afraid that she will need help disrobing. The young person who came to attend her was totally unsuitable."

He waited, but Mrs. Benson regarded him as if she had seen him stuff sixpence into the poor box. Parker, his face blank, offered no help. Danforth glanced over to the chair, and even at this distance he could see her heightened color. Suppressing a sigh, he addressed the housekeeper again. "I think that she should be put to bed."

Mrs. Benson drew in her breath. Small wonder Mr. Parker had not cared to disclose the purpose of this unusual interview! Blood rushed to her face as she prepared to share with his Grace her opinion of the females brought into this house, and the so-called dandies who accompanied them.

Danforth's voice had finally penetrated Elizabeth's sleep and she opened her eyes. Tears of relief came when she saw Mrs. Benson. The woman in the severely cut black worsted dress was so obviously respectable, she could be a reincarnation of her own nurse. Sanity was returning to Elizabeth's world, and she begged her for help. "Please, oh please, I do need you."

Her voice was neither steady nor loud, but in the

stillness of the room, it was as if she had shouted. The three turned. Mrs. Benson had not noticed her before; now she became so incensed that she started to tremble.

Outraged propriety exuding from each pore, the upright confronted the strumpet, her eyes minutely examining every inch of the shameless hussy. But the bedraggled hair, the miserable dress, and the feverish face with its large entreating eyes were not what she expected of a Mary Magdalene. Mrs. Benson's rage fell as quickly as it had grown, and pity for the poor, wretched creature took its place. Murmuring "sick was sick," she went to Elizabeth. The two men exchanged relieved looks and quietly left.

It was important that Elizabeth explain the situation to her new ally, but when she tried, only an incoherent jumble of words came out. The housekeeper gruffly reassured her, and while the sick woman could no longer understand what she said, she could feel the kindness, and relaxed. Mrs. Benson was aghast when she discovered Elizabeth's condition, and she tucked the robe tightly around her and pushed the large chair even closer to the fire.

Shaking her head, Mrs. Benson went into the adjoining dressing room to find a nightgown. One of the wardrobes was filled with frilly gowns, made to delight a woman's heart. The housekeeper was scandalized by the ungodly trappings of the harlot's trade; but, remembering the sick woman, she said a quick prayer and started to look through the skimpy, wanton things. Three complete searchings were needed before she could select a blue panne nightgown with blue and white rosebuds embroidered in shameless places.

The water had been brought up an hour ago and was only lukewarm, but she would not wait for an exchange. Gathering some towels from the commode, she took everything into the bedroom.

"There's nothing there for a decent woman!" Mrs. Benson announced as she set the water down by the fire. "Well, that's neither here nor there," she continued as she recollected what Elizabeth was. Talking all the while, she undressed Elizabeth and gently washed and dried her. Elizabeth quietly accepted the attention until the housekeeper started to remove the small gold locket hidden beneath her shift; rather than upset the sick woman unnecessarily, Mrs. Benson left it. She had hoped the wash would bring down the fever, but if anything Elizabeth felt hotter underneath the panne gown.

The tangled wet hair was rubbed, dried, and brushed, and although it looked better, Mrs. Benson bemoaned the absence of a nightcap. "Still, if I stand here wishing for things that ain't, it's not going to help you, now is it?" she asked and without waiting for an answer, she helped Elizabeth across to the bed. Fortunately the housekeeper was a strong woman, for Elizabeth was unable to walk.

"Silk sheets may be elegant," she said as she pulled back the covers and maneuvered Elizabeth into the big bed, "but they're not warm, that's for certain." Mrs. Benson tucked the covers over Elizabeth's shoulders and told her to get some sleep. "There's not a thing you can do anyway, so you might as well." Giving the covers a final adjustment, Mrs. Benson left. Elizabeth had closed her eyes and was into a fitful sleep before the housekeeper reached the door.

Chapter Six

When Lord Eversley planned the house party, he had no difficulty solving the household staff problem —he would make do—but the question of the cook was a different matter. Eversley was justly proud of his table; the French chef that he'd had for the last two months was an *artiste par excellence,* a virtuoso of the kitchen, *ne plus ultra* of his craft. To have a woman in charge of the hunting box's kitchen was as unthinkable as serving his guests indifferent food. His mind was made up; Pierre would have to come.

His chef was a highly temperamental man, as are all truly creative geniuses, so the subject of the house party was broached with care. For Pierre it was a difficult decision; he was torn between his great contempt for the provinces and pride in his art. In the end his pride, aided by the impressive purse offered by his employer, was allowed to overrule his prejudice, and Pierre made the long journey north to preside over the kitchen.

Once there he found what he expected; neither the kitchen nor the staff was up to his standard. He immediately started to rectify the situation, being extremely careful to explain each deficiency as he encountered it. The chef was accustomed to rule his kingdom as Louis XVI tried to rule his, but the continuous hysteria of his underlings, all local girls, was upsetting to his autocratic nature.

Both sides turned to the housekeeper, although it was outside her domain, constantly summoning her to arbitrate and soothe exacerbated feelings; and the Donnybrook Fair in the kitchen, coupled with her own considerable duties, kept Mrs. Benson hard pressed. Parker had been very fortunate to locate her quickly, and at a time when she could spare a few minutes.

Parker was waiting in the passage when she came out of the duke's chamber. He started to thank her for the attentions to his Grace's friend, but Mrs. Benson cut the expressions of gratitude short.

"Hate the sin, love the sinner. It's what I've been told to do all my life, and if my Lord can do it, why it won't kill me! No, that's not the poser. That poor thing needs some good care, for at least the next few hours." She went on to explain that because of the chaotic kitchen situation, she was at a loss to know what to suggest.

Poor Parker. He needed a moment to deal with the latest upset to his equanimity, and he turned to study the long upstairs hallway. His master evidently wished the woman to be well treated, but as he had interviewed Hoare and discovered how casually she had been acquired, the valet was not sure what the proper course should be. His Grace had been involved in some harebrained scrapes with certain lady birds, but that was way back in the duke's salad days. Best to tread very gently here.

Turning back to the housekeeper, he said, "My esteemed Mrs. Benson, I do think that if we were to ascertain how she is feeling now, before we contemplate further action, we might find that she only needs time to compose herself after the journey."

Mrs. Benson shrugged her shoulders. "You are certainly free, Mr. Parker, to make your own inspection. But seeing that miracles aren't everyday happenstances in the shires, I'd be much surprised if your observations any way differed from mine!" She nodded at him to open the door.

Elizabeth was oblivious to their entrance. Though she was lying on one of his lordship's new feather beds, she was tossing as if it were Margate shale. The fever had continued to rise and the pillow beneath her head was wet with perspiration. It was clear to the two observers that Mrs. Benson had not overstated the case.

Parker apologized. "You are entirely correct, Mrs. Benson," he said in a low voice. "She does need attention. I can remain here for the moment, but is there no one who could be spared from below? She does need a female beside her."

Mrs. Benson tried but could think of no one. "It's not that I don't want to help, for I do, but my own girls are in pieces just hearing all of the things from the kitchen. That Pierre uses his up like this lot upstairs uses tallow candles. There's always at least one having a fit in the pantry and another in the hall getting in the way of my housemaids. No, that's not the answer . . ." Her voice trailed off as a thought came to her.

"Now there might be one way," she slowly began. "Our Polly—that's my brother's youngest and lives not far—might as could come. She's quick and willing, for her being so young. I wouldn't allow her into this house at all now, as I've told her time and time again, but seeing that *you* are taking charge, Mr. Parker," and Mrs. Benson's voice became firm, "I know *you* will look after her. And that's all I can do. No matter how much I want to oblige, things are at fives and sixes below, and I've got to be getting back. I'll make up some sallow tea though. That'll help bring down the fever. I didn't hear any rattles in the lungs, so perhaps we can keep it from settling there. I'll send for Polly and soon as she comes, I'll bring her up myself." Mrs. Benson smiled, glad to have found a solution, as an unhappy Parker tried to feel grateful.

Later, when the duke reentered his chamber, he was nonplussed to find his valet sitting beside the bed watching the sleeping woman. "Is that confounded creature really sick?" he asked, keeping his voice low. He walked over for a closer look. A pungent odor struck him and he stopped. "What in the name of all that is holy is that smell?" he demanded.

The long-suffering Parker had raised his head when the door opened, but seeing it was only his master, he turned back to the patient. Taking a cloth out of the bowl of cold water on the table, he wrung it out and exchanged it for the warm one on Elizabeth's forehead. His voice was expressionless as he answered the duke's second question.

"That, sir, is what seems to be helping bring down the fever and calm her," and he indicated a large white cup on the table. "I believe Mrs. Benson called it sallow tea, which is a mixture of willow and gentian. One is from the bark and the other from the root, though I was imperfectly attending, so that I cannot assure you which is which. It has been efficacious though."

Before Danforth could give his opinion of rustic medicines, Elizabeth began to murmur, softly at first and then louder, until it became an intelligible phrase. Although her body was in England, her spirit was back in Iberia. "*Ayúdame, O ayúdame, por favor, ayúdame!*" she pleaded.

How could one simple woman be such a mixture? The duke moved closer and stood by the bed watching her. "But certainly she is English?" he asked.

"I would think so, sir," Parker answered, "but that, or something similar is what she does repeat."

Danforth considered the woman. Her bones were good. As she murmured her plea again, unaccustomed words of reassurance came to him, and he answered, "There, there, that's all right."

The cool English voice cut into Elizabeth's nightmares, halting them for the moment, and she became indignant. "That's what you say to a horse!" she said, and then slipped back into her hospital bed in Lisbon.

Danforth bristled. He could demonstrate kindness, but it should be valued. Parker felt it was propitious to assure his master that the situation at the sickbed was well in hand. His Grace might care to change into his dinner clothes, which were already laid out; for though town hours were observed, the time for dinner was near. The duke allowed himself to be persuaded and went to change.

Chapter Seven

The duke went down to join the others. What a muddle it was. He tried to be fair and admitted that she had not asked to come with him. But, if ever, at any time, another woman were found beneath the hooves of his horses, without a second thought he would order the coach on! They were waiting for him to go into dinner, and so, putting the woman upstairs out of his mind, he entered into the evening's pleasures.

Everyone was in a festive mood, the food was faultless, many agreeable stories were told, and all manner of games were played (mostly involving forfeits of kisses). After covers were removed, Maureen was helped onto the table where she danced a very spirited version of the hornpipe, which was loudly and well received. And, as none of the gentler sex cared to leave, they continued sitting around the table, zestfully consuming their port and brandy. There was nothing untoward in the evening. Danforth had sat through many similar—but never before alone.

No one noticed when he left. Parker met him in the upstairs hall and reported that Mrs. Benson's niece now was on duty; the fever had gone, and the patient was sleeping comfortably. This was not really what the duke had hoped to hear, but obviously their tête-à-tête would have to wait until morning. He turned and walked back to speak to his host.

The party was as he had left it, but Danforth no longer found it amusing. He would speak to Eversley, get another chamber, and retire for the night; but this was not to be. It took longer to extricate his host from Maureen's plump arms than it did to be told there were no more rooms.

"Ain't no others," said Eversley solemnly after he understood what Danforth was asking. "Only have six, y'know." He gave a lop-eared smirk as he dug his friend in the ribs. "Ain't as if we're married. Want to be together. Ha ha." Greshner-Blanginham shouted it was his turn to lead them in song as the duke tried to protest. Eversley patted him on the shoulder before rejoining the group. "Sorry about your friend not being up to snuff t'night. Have to go to it tomorrow!" To show he understood, Eversley led them all in a rousing Covent Garden ditty about a lover's plans for his mistress on the morrow.

Parker moved the sofa from the bedroom into the dressing room and made it up with proper sheets. As it had been made for an afternoon's rest, it would prove comfortable for an evening's repose. The duke retired with a bottle of port and an execrable temper.

Chapter Eight

Danforth, whose servants were as aphonic as dormice until he rose, was awakened by the sounds of female voices; the door between the two rooms not having been properly closed. Thus it was a very irascible man who found his Ottoman silk dressing gown and threw it on, thrust his feet into the Turkish slippers, pushed open the bedroom door, and strode in.

His entrance was unnoticed, for the two women were intent on their dispute. His guest was sitting on the side of the bed demanding her clothes; the young maid, mindful of instructions, was trying to persuade her to lie down again.

"Damn it, woman, are you always doing something?" His voice had the desired effect; they stopped talking. "Not a very restful sort, are you?" He was as cutting as possible. "Do you know what time it is?"

They had turned to stare at the tall man in his jade-green dressing gown. His body was well proportioned and pleasing to feminine tastes, his bearing that of a man accustomed to authority. He had done no more than run his hands through his black hair, but it appeared fashionably disarrayed. Were he in a different temper and his face not so stern, he would immediately be called handsome. As he was now, he looked formidable.

The niece blushed as she curtsied and then, remembering what her aunt had said about the gentlemen, she scurried out of the room. Elizabeth, who had hoped that what little she recalled of late yesterday was only the product of the fever, remained sitting on the bed, looking at him.

Danforth found his humor restored by the attractive body artfully revealed by the soft draperies of the blue nightgown. Small feet, shapely legs, softly rounding thighs and hips, hard belly, full well-rounded breasts, that warmly sensual mouth, her straight red nose—damn it all, the woman had a cold!

Elizabeth watched his eyes move slowly up her body. She might be a horse on the block at Tattersall's. Would he inspect her teeth too? She shivered, then quickly put herself back into bed, holding the sheets over her shoulders. Their eyes met. His showed interest, and she lowered hers.

He approached, made a small bow, and said, "Good morning, my charming lady. Please do accept my regrets for the uncivil manner in which I greeted you this morning. It did, however, clear the room, you must admit." He smiled very nicely at her. "I hesitate, I confess, to suggest that we talk, for the last time I proposed it, you became ill. I do trust you are feeling better this morning?" His customary good fortune had not deserted him, in spite of last night and her cold. And she was shy, which was to his liking.

Elizabeth managed a low, "Perfectly well, sir," then had to blow her nose. It was true; she did feel better than yesterday, but were she only in some other place, she would be content to lie in bed. She was weak after the fever and ached all over. Her head was stuffed, her right ear hurt, and her nose dripped; but these ailments were not her paramount concern.

Ever since waking, she had tried to sort through the memories, shifting out the obvious phantasms (Spain, the bear pit, capture by buccaneers, etc.), yet the bits which remained were very disturbing.

Now to be confronted by this imperious man who so evidently wished to exercise seigniory over her—Elizabeth was frightened, but determined she would not show it. He was nothing more than another obstacle to overcome.

The door opened and Parker entered with a large silver tray laden with tea and various other dishes for two. "Good morning, sir. Good morning, madam." He bent his head toward each in turn. "I do apologize for Polly, who is unaccustomed to service." He put the tray down on the table in front of the fire.

"May I find madam's robe" he asked, and without waiting for a reply, went into the dressing room, returning with a deep blue Genoa velvet robe over his arm and a pair of blue velvet slippers in his hand. "I hesitate about the slippers. They may be a trifle loose," he said as he placed the robe on the foot of the bed and the slippers on the floor beneath. "If there is nothing else, sir?" he asked and, receiving a negative reply, bowed again and exited.

When the door was shut, Danforth walked over and picked up the gown. "My dear, do permit me," he said as he approached, holding the robe.

This was not a time for weak hearts; boldness would carry her through. "No doubt it is a nicety, sir, but I am not accustomed to receive in my chamber. If you would be so kind—" She was going to tell him to leave, but he held up his hand and stepped back two paces.

"Then you must allow me the honor of presenting myself. I am Edward Charles Augustus Frederick Rawling, Duke of Danforth, at your service." His bow was worthy of Queen Charlotte. She said nothing. "Ah but, my very correct lady, you have not returned the courtesy." He was enjoying her shyness. It enhanced her femininity.

She tried to sound as toplofty as possible. "I count myself fortunate then. I am invaded by a peer and not a postboy." He continued to smile at her; she would have to try a new tack. "Sir, we are not children. It is time for plain speaking!"

"My dear, I am in accord. It will be far better when we are frank with each other. Last night was too hurried, too interrupted to have you feel at ease, I know, and I am sorry. I did not plan it so, but events overtook us, it seems. This morning we shall start anew. Part of our pleasure will be in the discovery of each other. I shall be gentle, never fear."

To cover her feelings, Elizabeth blew her nose again. One fragment that had seemed too outrageous, too terrible (the product of a woman's worst fears) now was affirmed as fact. He had taken his pleasure with her—and would do so again! Now was not the time to cry, not in front of him; tears were a luxury here. Her remorse would be dealt with later. There was the rest of her life for regrets. Now escape was uppermost in her mind. But, had she felt enjoyment? one small part of her insisted on asking. For what a sad thing to be ruined with no real recollection of it. Elizabeth took hold of herself. As if it mattered! Her fists tightened as she readied herself to confront him.

"Sir, let me speak boldly. You talk of gentleness. Rape is not a gentle sport. It will have to be that, before I submit." She was pale, but there was determination in her low voice.

Danforth frowned. Did she wish to be taken violently? Ah women! May he persuade her it would be too much for today. He became his most winning. "My dear, I would not recommend too athletic a lovemaking this morning. I am sure you are not quite recovered from yesterday, and I do not wish to see you prostrate again. Only consider: I should chase you around the room, you fleeing just before my grasp, dodging the chairs, around the tables, even under the bed, but at last I catch you, falling on top of you. I throw off your garments and mine—and to what end? To do that which we could do so much more comfortably in the bed?" He had tried to make the idea appear as ludicrous as possible, but she did not return his smile, so he continued, "However, later if you still desire a more strenuous form, your wish is but my command."

Elizabeth had listened to his recital without showing the panic that she felt, but his last statement was too much. In a bitter voice she asked, "I may choose any form of debauchery I desire? Really you are too kind, sir."

The duke did not find her shyness as attractive as it first had been, but he tried to reassure her. "Why, I protest, my fair one. Plain speaking, even ribaldry, to be sure. But to call our pleasure, our desire, a debauchery is cruel, an untruth worthy of a Scottish divine. Come, my dear, our natures are passionate, a very part of us. We wish to have a mutual enjoyment of each other. There is nothing amiss in that!"

"There is no joy in me, sir. There is repulsion, and horror, and . . ." Her voice was steady, but her eyes were intent upon the bedpost.

"Look at me!" he commanded, and her grave eyes came up to his. "You are a woman, not a maid, and I addressed you as such. Forgive me if I have frightened you by speaking bluntly. It was not my intention; instead I wished to still your fears." He reached for her hand as he said, "Do trust me—you may."

In another second he would touch her, and words poured out of her innermost heart. "Did I enjoy it when you took me last night?"

His hand jerked back. "Good God, woman!" he roared. "I did not touch you! What do you take me for!"

"Well, sir," she countered, as upset as he. "What do you take me for?"

Each wondered if the other were mad as they warily considered the other. This was one of the few times in his life Danforth had taken a header, and he became very thoughtful.

"My dear," he began slowly, "I am afraid there has been a small misunderstanding."

"Misunderstanding—God's blood!" Elizabeth snapped. "There has been nothing but chaos!" She still was confused but relieved; and in her relief anger came to the front. She would tear him limb from limb—and then think.

"Ah, yes, to be sure," Danforth answered and went over to the table and returned with two cups of tea. He put them down on the bedside table, pulled up a chair, and sat down. "You may safely take it. I am not going to ravish you. However, we do have some things that must be settled. Now, what exactly do you remember of last night?"

Her anger fell as she had to admit the truth. "Very little, I fear. I truly was not well. Not that it excuses what may have happened, but . . ."

"What may have happened!" He could shake this female. "Do you, or do you not, recollect our embrace in the coach?"

"To some extent." Her voice was very low.

"Woman . . ." Inexplicably words failed him.

Seeing his discomposure, Elizabeth pressed her momentary advantage. "Well, sir, do you kidnap every female you meet?" Her eyes were sad no longer but flashed with her readiness to do battle.

"Don't be completely witless! Of course not!" He was angry at her stupidity. He was extremely careful in the selection of his women. Now this baggage twisted everything, and to score a point of his own, he asked, "And do you make a practice of dalliance with every gentleman?"

Elizabeth blushed and looked away. How ashamed she felt, and rightly so, but when she was ready to speak fairly of this, he was regarding her in such a censorious fashion that she forgot her own contrition. "Don't try the merry-andrew on me, sir!" she ordered. "I was exhausted; you tried to run me down! And why did you take me in your arms?"

And at one point he had thought her shy! "Because, you goose, you were on the point of freezing to death, that is why! The next time, I promise, I shall leave you!"

"Thank you, please do!" Her head was equally high.

Their voices had risen with their tempers, and they faced each other squarely, each trying to stare the other down. This lasted for several moments, and then Elizabeth's sense of proportion reasserted itself.

"This is a profitless exercise, sir. Now, since we both agree you had no trouble bringing me here, may I suggest you will have no problem taking me back?" His expression of outrage made her burst out laughing, and after a few seconds he joined in with his own rueful laugh.

"And put you back into the snow in front of my coach? No, you were right." He continued soberly now. "My actions were hasty. And I am afraid it is no longer that simple, my dear. You have stayed the night."

That was an uncomfortable fact, Elizabeth admitted, but not that it was the most important. "We are having our morning tea *en famille* too," she said. "Oh, there is no need to be gothic! I have not been ruined, and I wish to leave. I would prefer to do it in as inconspicuous a manner as possible, however . . ." Her voice trailed off and she shrugged her shoulders.

Danforth studied her with great care. She was not the usual sort, certainly. Lamentable temper, yes, but to face such a situation this well—no, this woman was not of the common mold.

"Would you have me cry, sir? I am convinced that it would be most uncomfortable with my cold. And I do not think it would serve a purpose."

"Madam, I salute you." He took her hand and kissed it. "You are a brave woman. Now, be braver still, my dear, and tell me who you are, and why you were on the road so late." There was admiration in his smile.

Elizabeth found his kindness more disturbing than his disdain, but she made her voice matter-of-fact as she answered him. "I am Elizabeth Campbell and, as I am widowed, I answer to no one but myself." A small sigh escaped. "As to why I was there, I was on an errand of mercy, or so I thought, for a distant kinswoman. As she did not expect me, she cannot miss me."

"But your baggage?"

"At the White Horse, the inn at the crossroads. It was only a small bag."

The duke got up. "I think the first thing we can do is send for your bag. What I do not enjoy is the predicament in which I have placed you."

There was a little "Neither do I" behind him as he went to the bell rope and pulled it. "What an

50

excellent idea," Elizabeth announced. "We shall have action at last. Do send for it in your own coach. Tell all where I have been!" She blew her nose loudly.

Danforth saw the wisdom in her words, but Parker entered before he could rethink, and to gain a moment he asked what the weather was like.

"We are snowed in for the present, sir."

The effect on his listeners was all the impassive valet could wish, and he had their complete attention. "The snow, it seems, continued to fall during the night and is falling still. Mrs. Benson assures me that a plentitude of supplies has been laid in, for this is known to occur every three or so years. There is no cause for alarm."

"No cause for alarm!" Elizabeth repeated. "Are you mad? What am I going to do?" She looked from master to servant for the answer.

Parker did not move an inch, but Danforth made a decision. "My dear, I think it would be helpful to take Parker into our confidence. He is totally trustworthy." Elizabeth snorted, but the duke ignored her and turned to his valet. "You see, Parker, there has been a small misunderstanding, and it seems that madam"—he made Elizabeth a small bow—"is not exactly what—"

Would the man never reach his point? Elizabeth spoke. "To be blunt, Parker, I am not one of his doxies!"

Danforth immediately protested. "Never did I take you for one, my dear. Rather shall we say, a knowledgeable woman of the town was what I considered."

"As you found me on a country road, I realize your perceptions are finer than mine," Elizabeth said acidly. Without desiring to do so, they had fallen into argument again.

Parker spoke before his master could reply. "I understand then," and he bowed to them. "There has been a misunderstanding."

"Yes, that's it."

"Yes, exactly."

"Good, that's settled," the duke said. "And there is no problem with abandoning your bag, for the moment only, for there are clothes enough for several in the dressing room." Elizabeth blew her nose on the damp handkerchief.

Parker went into the dressing room, returning with a fresh pile of handkerchiefs, which he presented to Elizabeth. He was dismissed but, before leaving, he addressed Elizabeth. "Anyway that I may be of service, ma'am, please do not hesitate to call upon me." With small bows to them both, he went out.

Danforth was thoughtful, "You know, my dear, you seem to have made a hit with Parker. He has never said that before to any of my friends—much less done anything for them."

Elizabeth could not help smiling. "I daresay it is because he did not approve of your irregular connections. He probably has better morals than his master."

Danforth smiled back at her. "All good servants have, my dear."

Chapter Nine

"I really must commend you on your good sense in not going down to dinner last night," the duke said as Elizabeth finished off the last piece of torte, one of the dishes on the morning tray which Danforth himself had carried over to the bedside table. He'd persuaded Elizabeth to stay in bed and put on the robe so that she could sit up without clutching the covers to her. "Difficult to eat lying down, my dear." It was well she did so, for even he was impressed by her appetite. Not that it was such a wonderful thing, she'd pointed out, for she'd not eaten since a bowl of soup and some bread at one of the stage stops yesterday.

"You are not known to the other guests," he continued, "nor to our host, for that matter. We just might be able to carry this off. But you must promise not to leave this room and allow no one but your gawky Polly and Parker to attend you."

For all of Elizabeth's interest in the tray, her mind had been trying for a solution, but nothing immediate came to mind. It appeared best to follow his suggestions and trust him, at least until the roads cleared. After what had passed, why did she believe she might put faith in this domineering *hidalgo*? Oddly it was not because of his expressions of contrition, but rather because he had a sense of humor.

To further this conclusion, she licked the last crumb from her fingers and said, "I must warn you, if it is ransom you are now thinking of, I have but a small annuity. May I suggest, sir, that if you truly have taken to the life of crime, either you did not choose the victim or crime well. I am not sure which." She appeared puzzled.

The duke sat at ease, enjoying her. Here was a woman who found herself in an abominable position, full of pluck. "Then, my dear," he said, "I shall do as you suggest, and rethink my crime again." He sat, his brows furrowed for a moment, then straightened up and said, "Ah, yes, upon reconsidering, it shall be your body after all." He laughed at her startled expression, then became very serious. "Listen to me, Elizabeth. I do not ruin decent women. No hint of scandal shall ever be attached to your name. On that you have my word."

The confirmation made her feel a little teary and, instead of answering, she just nodded and blew her nose. He proposed to dress and then discover the situation for himself, not that he doubted his valet. He suggested that Elizabeth would care to spend the day in bed, and to her surprise she found herself agreeing with him. With everything settled, he promised to send Polly in to her and left.

Polly entered to clear the tray. Gawky was a good word for the not quite fifteen-year-old. Two braids on the top of her head framed a trusting, open face, making her appear even younger. Her dark, high-necked wool dress covered thin limbs, and her movements were awkward, but she was kindly and willing.

Mrs. Benson had given instructions that Elizabeth was to be bathed again and helped into a fresh gown, and that the sheets were to be changed. Elizabeth appreciated the attention, but this time she preferred to wash herself. The new gown was also of panne, beige instead of blue, with fragile lace inserts from the neck to the middle of her breasts. From Polly's scandalized face, Elizabeth knew it was most revealing; whether it was attractive on her, she could not know. An outer robe, also beige with lace at the hem and sleeves, was put on the bedside chair. Elizabeth sat by the fire while the bed was changed and was very glad to be helped back into it, for the little activity had tired her. She quickly fell into a dreamless sleep.

A couple of hours later she was awakened by a scratching at the door. It was Danforth, and she bade him enter. He was informally, yet appropriately dressed for the house party. His coat was a brown superfine double-breasted one, tailored by Weston. His shirt collars were high pointed, enclosing the starched neckcloth done in a style known as the Danforth Fall. Striped waistcoat, with nankeen trousers, and highly polished brown shoes completed the outfit. A signet ring on his right hand was his only jewelry. To an inch he appeared what he was, a discriminating man of fashion.

She smiled in welcome, and he returned it as he came to her. She need not have worried; the beige gown was as becoming as the blue one had been. Although her nose was still red, her blue eyes were clear. The sleep had done her good. He took her hand, kissed it, and complimented her. "My dear, you look better."

While Elizabeth felt it important that they be on a friendly footing, she did not feel an intimate one was prudent. So ignoring the frank appreciation in his eyes, she said, "Sir, I do object to being called 'my dear'; I do not find it seemly. And please do hand me my robe."

"Forgive me," he answered contritely. "It shall be as you wish—Elizabeth."

"Sir, you make fun of me!"

"On the contrary, my dear lady—that is sufficiently neutral not to cause alarm—I would never make jest of you. But you too must remember that my name is Edward, not 'sir.' " He smiled so nicely that she had to respond.

"That's better," he said as he picked up the robe and helped her into it before sitting down next to her. "I shall now make my report. It is as Parker said, no better, no worse. It makes no difference to the others, for the games they are playing are best enjoyed indoors. But for us . . ." He spread his hands open.

Elizabeth could not help a small moan. She had hoped the confident valet had been wrong. Danforth took her hands. "My dear Elizabeth. Yes, it is proper for us to use our Christian names. We are and shall be sharing this apartment for the while." She was staring up at him with such an appealing face that he wanted to do more than hold her hands to comfort her. He again realized it was not going to be simple.

She soon took her hands away and blew her nose. "I am sorry, sir, Edward. I shan't be a ninny again, never fear, but what can we do?" Her face was controlled but the eyes were wistful.

"Well, for one thing, we can decide how we can best amuse ourselves," he said, and he laughed at the immediate look of horror that came to her face. "My dear, are you not an advocate of plain speaking? It was cards that I was about to suggest."

"It's too much to suppose that just because you are a duke, you are a gentleman too!" she snapped. "Oh, let it be cards." She knew she was being pettish, but she didn't care.

Parker was sent for a couple of packs and amazingly the time passed easily. She had partnered her father, and while the duke was a better player than he, she was good enough to make the games interesting. He decided she must be introduced to the rest of the guests and did so, telling all kinds of scurrilous tales about them. Elizabeth tried to be scandalized, but could not, for he told the stories well. Still she was thankful she did not have to meet them, although he assured her she would enjoy the gentlemen—though perhaps in another setting.

After their meal he asked that she tell him more about herself. While she had shared several stories about her father when they were playing cards, she had not mentioned Ian. Now would be a good time, she felt, to talk about her husband; it would help keep the duke's considerable charm in proper perspective.

They had almost grown up together, for Ian had spent the holidays at his aunt's house on the other side of the park from the rectory. He had been welcomed into their house, first to share lessons with Elizabeth, and then for himself, as the son the Rector never had. There was a bond, a closeness between them, and they always knew they would marry. But when Ian came to claim her, proud and resplendent in his new uniform, he learned that her father had fallen ill two days before. It had come suddenly, taking the strong, upright Rector and twisting him, leaving his left side paralyzed but his mind intact. There was never a question but that Elizabeth would stay. Her father, who had loved and cared for them both, must come first now. There was another paralyzing bout two years later, leaving his body completely worthless, but again not touching the great mind. Elizabeth read to him, debated with him, listened to him, stayed with him, and closed his eyes when he died.

"It was time, then, to resume our own lives," Elizabeth continued. "I went to London after the funeral, carrying with me my father's love and blessing for us both, and we were married by Special License. I had always been Ian's, but now that we were joined under law, Ian could not bear to leave me. He was afraid, it was almost a presentiment, that we would not have much time left together. There were very few wives who accompanied their husbands; it was difficult to obtain all the necessary permissions, but at last I had them and I went to Spain too. Had Ian been less of a leader, less brave, he would not have been Ian. He was frequently mentioned in dispatches. I was proud of him. I would not let myself fear."

She stopped. She could not describe his death, not speak, at least this moment, of the assault on Cuidad Rodrigo. Perhaps another time.

"You would not think me sensible," she slowly began again, "if you had known me after he was killed. I hated both God and the French—and myself. I suppose I was mad, but it did not show—at least to the world. It was the end of all my hopes, of me. There was no reason to live."

Elizabeth stared out of the far window, not seeing the winter Leicestershire landscape, not present in England at all. She had never before been able to speak of this, never been able to reveal this much of her own grief and heartache. It was painful, but recalling herself to her surroundings, she realized it was not as distressing as she had thought it would be. She turned to her companion and with a small, tight smile, begged his pardon.

"For that is done," she said firmly. "My life is starting anew. I am ready to meet my future, and it will be what I determine. I do not care to remarry, but I plan to contribute myself to the betterment of those less fortunate. I shall be content."

"You are to be commended for your courage, Elizabeth," he said gravely, "but would it not be more agreeable to enter society?" She gave him a scornful look, but he took no notice, "No, you could, you know. Your background is good, and there must be many who would welcome you for the sake of your husband. My aunts, for example, would be happy to sponsor you."

"Oh, how lovely, Edward! With that backing I should go to all of the balls and ride sedately in the park—only at the proper times, of course. No! I am not in the marriage mart, and if I am not, why, it all seems a waste of time. If I were a man, I would be interested in one of the Ministries, or private secretary to one of the Members of Parliament. There are many conditions I should like to change." The duke looked skeptical. "No, people in your condition do not know what the world is like. Oh, no doubt you made a Grand Tour and speak several languages, but you only know people of your own class and all of you have too much free time and much too much money. Most people have neither, yet they are decent and are trying to improve their own lot—and that of their children. I should like to help." She had forgotten her distress as she tried to bring him to sense.

"Then," responded the duke firmly—some of her words had stung—"you should certainly marry a man of influence. The little you might accomplish alone would be mere trifles. Charitable persons usually receive more benefits themselves than do the objects of their so-called beneficiences. Why waste yourself?"

It was as well for their developing rapport that Parker entered to close the curtains. Danforth informed her that he would do himself the honor of dining with her in the room, and he again forbid her to leave the bed. He would change and then spend awhile with the others before joining her. He took his leave very correctly.

Elizabeth lay down, and after she was able to think of things other than Danforth's benighted opinions, she rested. Polly brought up hot water when she came to help Elizabeth freshen up before dinner. While her hair was being brushed, Elizabeth was conscious of how easily she had become used to service, how pleasant it was. Danforth entered, having changed into black skin-tight pantaloons which showed his legs to advantage. Elizabeth had been used to the officer's gatherings in the Peninsula and the company of attractive, well-turned-out men, but this man, she decided, would shine anywhere.

He allowed no constraint between them, choosing topics of conversation that would both interest and amuse her. Had Elizabeth seen Trevithick's, "Catch-me-who-can" some years ago in London? He described the scene as all classes of people gathered to watch the marvelous invention. Had she read of Burckhardt's discovery of the Great Temple of Abu Simel last year? He had read the Swiss's reports. Was Plough Monday celebrated at her home? He had been on one of his estates in Anglia three years before when they dragged the ploughs from door to door soliciting plough money for their feast. Then on to mumming plays and sword dances and when they found they held the same opinion of Scott's romantic poems, the rest of the evening was pure enjoyment.

It was very late when the duke said good night and retired to his dressing room. Elizabeth lay thinking of the contrasting facets of the duke: handsome, personable, intelligent, a sense of humor; but autocratic, proud, stubborn, and holding antiquated notions. How different from Ian, but one could not compare the two. There was an excitement about

Edward. Elizabeth would think of other things. Clarice came to mind. Poor girl: the cause of Elizabeth's journey and totally forgotten. But if she herself could not travel, neither could her cousin, and so as Elizabeth fell into sleep, the features of a certain dark-haired man drifted in to join her.

Chapter Ten

The next morning Elizabeth woke up feeling almost herself again. Her cold was much better, with no trace of pain in her ear; the stuffiness in her head was almost gone, and her body was refreshed. She stretched catlike in response to the warmth of the room. Then panic started to rise as her brain began to work; but when she contrasted today with yesterday—to awake in a strange room, alone, frightened, and sick—she realized that indeed it was a fine day! She now knew what must be faced, and even if she had to walk through the snow today, she would manage. Polly opened the curtains of the bed and wished her a shy good morning.

"And how is the weather today?" Elizabeth asked, smiling at her wide-eyed, young handmaiden.

"Oh, ma'am, it is a bit better than before, but it won't stay that way long, so my aunt says. It's not snowing, but it's still dark and gloomy out and there's more to come," Polly answered.

Then there is nothing to do, Elizabeth concluded, but to rest and allow herself to be a hedonist. How comfortable to be able to do what one wishes, and have such an elegant room to be indolent in. She smiled when she thought for what purpose it had been reserved. It was such a splendid sickroom. Now here she was, ordinary Elizabeth Campbell, with purple and fine linen, except that purple would clash with the rest of the room and the sheets were of silk. No one alive would not enjoy such comfort!

She would be dressed today. Her own dress had been washed and ironed, Polly informed her, and was hanging in one of the wardrobes. The wardrobes, however, were in the dressing room, which also contained a duke. (And what an absurd thing that was; as if one had dukes in the next room as one had pigeon pie!)

Elizabeth got up, put on the velvet robe and slippers and took one of the chairs by the fire. Tea and hot chocolate were on the waiting tray, and she let Polly pour a cup of chocolate and then dismissed her. Elizabeth wanted to sit and look in the fire and think.

She was soon joined by Danforth, who wished her a good day and thanked her for not waking him with the cacophony of yesterday. He complimented her on her health, determined that she had received the same report on the weather, and poured himself a cup of tea and sat down. They were a very domestic grouping, both in their robes, sitting in front of the fire, sipping their early morning cups, and Elizabeth was conscious of it.

"I'm not really in a funk, but I do feel improper." Danforth chose to misinterpret her remark. "Not a thing to trouble yourself about," he said reassuringly. "Most becoming, my dear, most becoming."

"That wasn't at all what I meant. I was not casting for a compliment. I know the robe is beautiful."

"Most attractive on you. Your colors." He nodded his agreement.

"Must you be impossible!" Elizabeth was half laughing, half provoked. "If you must know, all this makes me feel like a fallen woman."

"You don't approve of the style?" He inspected her. "Not a fault. It is the latest, you know, or so Madame Annette assured me herself when I chose it."

"You are a provoking man! Will you not be serious this morning?"

"Elizabeth, you are at your best when you are in a passion. Timidity does not become you. Did you wish to quarrel about whose bedchamber it is, or is it more proper to receive in the bed, as you did yesterday, or sitting in the chair, as you are this morning?"

She laughed. He was correct; there was no point in brooding about things which could not be changed at the moment. He joined in her laughter.

"That's Elizabeth! You looked so solemn for a while. Come, have another cup of chocolate. You would not wish to leave any." He poured the remainder into her cup and stretched his legs out in front of him.

Did Elizabeth ride? She did and the conversation turned to horses and to hunting, for the duke and Eversley rode with the Quorn. Eversley was a true Melton man, a buck of the first water, and his hunting box was filled with friends during the season. If the weather were better, and if she did not have a cold, and if it were possible to expose her to the others, he would enjoy showing her some of Eversley's hunters or going for a ride, for their host could mount her on one of his hacks.

During the season every hotel, inn, and country house was filled with the Quality as well as the riffraff from all over the world, for this was the most famous hunting country in England. They hunted during the day and spent the evening larking, having midnight steeplechases, parties, balls, cockfights, drinking, and almost anything else that one might imagine. One slept when the season was over.

The duke said he would dress first and wander around the house so that Elizabeth might use the dressing room. "Not that another soul will be up yet, but it will allow me to demonstrate how thoughtful I can be." But it was another hour before he left her, as he remembered that he had not told her about Johnny Morris's wager with Longfield in which they bought every chicken in Melton Mowbray market and raced them, Longfield's scattering throughout the county aided by the judicious use of a peashooter by one of Morris's younger supporters.

When the duke had finished in the dressing room, Elizabeth entered. It was almost as large as the bedchamber and decorated in the same style. The fireplace was a little smaller, though, and hanging in place of the mirror of the other room was a painting of Paris judging the three goddesses. Elizabeth regarded it critically. It was of the Italian school and a robust work, not to her taste, but then this was a gentleman's establishment.

The sofa was next to the fire and it eased her conscience to find it very comfortable; she carefully smoothed out the imprint of her body in the carefully made bed. There was a rosewood dressing table between the windows, a chest of drawers, a commode, and two very large wardrobes against the bedroom wall.

Polly directed her to one of the wardrobes and opened it. The contrast between Elizabeth's serviceable gray dress and the others was almost too much. All of those lovely clothes, of the latest mode, from the most exclusive modistes—all just for a mistress! The embroideries, the laces, the expensive fabrics, even the shifts were exquisitely done.

The other woman must be blond too for the colors suited Elizabeth. She had wondered about her, her age, what she might be like, why he found her of interest. Was there the ease between them that Elizabeth enjoyed with Danforth? Could they talk, or was it only a physical pleasure? To Elizabeth's knowledge she had never met a woman of that class. What a different world the duke moved in, going with ease back and forth between the *ton* and the *demimonde*.

Elizabeth felt reckless and she selected a pale green silk dress with deep green contrasts around the neck and sleeve ends. She was happy to discover that her own waist was two inches smaller than the unknown woman's. It was but a minor task for Polly to correct it. There were no shoes; Elizabeth only had her boots, but she had a choice of black, brown, or white satin slippers, and she chose the brown.

She elected to have her hair braided and wound softly on top of her head. The mirror told her she looked very well (in spite of her cold), and when Danforth entered, he agreed. She smiled, acknowledging his appreciation, and he bowed and kissed her hand.

Still holding her hand, he remarked, "My dear, you must decide what our role is to be. If you truly desire nothing but friendship between us, do not continue to regard me in such a delightful manner."

"What rubbish, sir!" she said, pulling her hand away, but his look was so frankly appraising that she chose to blow her nose. His comment had been just, she admitted to herself, and she looked up and told him so. "That was fair, Edward."

"I know. This is probably the basis for the unwritten rule not to seduce good women. They do not know how to play the game."

Lunch was brought up and afterward they played cards again. When Elizabeth discovered that he had been cheating to let her win, she roundly told him off.

"Your command of the language is very good, Elizabeth—if a trifle unusual for a gentlewoman," he said when she had finished.

"Edward, you display a shocking lack of sensibility for one so wellborn. '`Tis virtue, and not birth, that makes us noble.' "

"Ah, but my dear, Shakespeare has a different emphasis. 'He was not born to shame: Upon his brow shame is ashamed to sit.' "

"One can find points for both sides of an argument in his writings! That was from *Romeo and Juliet,* wasn't it? Romeo was never an interesting hero to me; too young, brash, and wanting his own way too much."

"And then, who are your heroes?"

"Well, Richard III was a man whose passion I could understand, even if I did not overlike him."

They debated the merits of Richard, Macbeth, and Falstaff, wishing there were copies of the plays in the house, for both enjoyed reading aloud. Danforth attempted one of Hamlet's speeches, but Elizabeth did not think it entirely correct.

She had been taught by her father. Latin and Greek were to be mastered, histories were to be read and discussed. That she learned to cook and sew was only due to the insistence of her old nurse, for it had not occurred to the Rector that his daughter might find these skills useful. She became her father's hostess when she was older, presiding over a table where everything from the 1802 Factory Act to Vergil to Bourne's *Antiquitates Vulgares; or the Antiquities of the Common People* were discussed. They had lived in the country, but her father's friends had been men of learning.

"It was not the usual education for a girl, but it suited me," Elizabeth said reflectively.

How different was the duke's education, with its stress on refinement, not knowledge. First the tutors at home, then on to Eton and Oxford, followed by the Grand Tour. When he returned to England, he was considered an educated man and ready to enter society. A gentleman was expected to have an acquaintance with the classics, music, and the arts, but not a love for them. He had dissembled in the beginning, keeping his interests in books and art to himself; now that he was older, he did what he pleased. His collection of Etruscan artifacts was the best in the country. He bought Flemish and Italian paintings as well as English ones. *Ars longa, vita brevis;* art is long, life is short.

For one who had so much, whose life was what he ordered it, he did not seem a contented man. Elizabeth tried to concentrate on her toilette rather than consider why she felt sorry for Danforth. She was to use the dressing room first while he went down for a glass with Eversley and the others. All of the décolletages on the evening frocks were much lower than she was used to. Either mistresses were less conservative than wives or she had been out of the world too long—or both. She settled on a sable brown watered silk which made her look very handsome and a woman of the world.

Her hair presented a problem. The fashion was for short hair; hers was long. It would have to be a half braid for the front, piled on her head with the back hanging down, and Polly did a creditable job with it.

The duke told her how well she looked when he came for dinner and she thanked him, but neither refined on it. Dinner was served and as they ate, Danforth regaled her with the latest stories, *on dits,* and news. After dinner he remained with her, saying he preferred her company if she would have him. It was a comfortable evening for them both.

Four days passed in this fashion, with the duke and Elizabeth continually discovering things in common—in harmony most of the time. He spent less and less time with his friends. Although the others kept themselves occupied, the constant association was beginning to wear thin, for their routine needed to be varied with walks, rides, or other diversions. Consequently the gentlemen gambled more and drank more, and the women became a little surly, and drank more too. As expected, there were lover's quarrels, but as the days and nights went on, they took longer to resolve.

The other women had closely questioned Maureen's maid, but as her only interview with Elizabeth had been that first night, no one could comprehend Danforth's continued interest. On the evening of the fifth day all insisted that he join them for dinner, even if his friend were still sick and could not. He would rather have been with Elizabeth but felt it wiser to agree to go down.

At the table the conversation was uninspired, much of it directed to Danforth, joshing him about his obsession, but the drinking was steady. He allowed his glass to be filled more than he wished, but his head was good and he was able to hold his own through the interminable dinner.

Chapter Eleven

For the evening Elizabeth changed into a deep blue faille dress with rows of small horizontal pleats running between the low neckline to the high waist. Polly brushed her hair and divided it into five parts, twisting each into a coil and intertwining the coils into a becoming crown on Elizabeth's head. Parker arrived to serve her dinner. He had now organized an efficient system. The trays were carried up by maids and deposited onto a table outside the bedroom door for Parker to bring in and serve.

Dinner was to Pierre's usual standards, but Elizabeth picked at the partridge soufflé, ate only a little of the braised calves's tongues, and merely tasted the saddle of lamb with soubise sauce, and some hot ham mousse with Madeira sauce; she rejected the two soups, the eel matelote, the poached salmon with white-wine sauce, the chickens stuffed with forcemeat and its kidney and sweetbread garnish, the topside of veal with jelly, the two patés, and the vegetables. For sweets, she took a little of the fruit croûte and some charlotte.

Elizabeth was lonely. She knew she was being childish, but she was lonely. How spoiled she had become in the last few days; how she had come to enjoy Edward's attentions. His first duty was to his friends; she would be foolish were she to feel neglected. Now if she were wise, she would think ahead to what her life would be when she was able to leave the hunting box. She must scrutinize her plans once more and make further decisions concerning her own future, instead of feeling sad she did not have the company of a certain gentleman. But as she slowly sipped the deep red wine, she wondered how her host obtained it, for it surely was French. Her thoughts went to the dinner below. Rather than reflect on that, she called to mind some of the tales he had told her, stories of his own upbringing and travels, and she reviewed discussions they had had ranging from the politics of the Royal Academy to the best way to prepare hare.

She did not get ready for bed, as Danforth had promised to look in before retiring, but it was late before she heard him at the door, and her relief and happiness at seeing him showed in her welcome. He had intended to give her good night from the doorway, for he was a bit foxed, but the warmth of her greeting called him in. All he was going to do then was kiss her hand and bid her sleep, but her upturned face declared such joy and invited him to share it, that it drew his lips down.

It was a gentle loving kiss, acknowledging their delight in each other, a happy kiss which came from their regard; but slowly it changed, growing into a demand for more. He pulled her up into his arms, roughly pressing her body to his, claiming her lips for his own, hungry for her, wanting her, wanting her now.

He picked her up in his arms and carried her the few steps to the bed, his eyes flashing desire as they held hers. He began very softly to explore her face with his lips and hands, and then very deliberately moved down her neck, down to her breasts. Encountering her locket, he thrust it aside, but it broke Elizabeth's passion. She wrenched herself away to the other side of the bed.

He came for her, but she put one hand out to stop him as the other held the locket. "No, Edward, no! Ian . . ."

"And what does your dead husband have to do with us, now and here?" he asked, his voice harsh. "If the damned locket you're clutching reminds you of him, I'll show you how simple it is to take it off." He would be brutal; he wanted her, and he wanted her to admit her passion too. "Unless, of course, while I was making love to you, you were pretending I was he?"

Elizabeth had thought of, had wanted no other person in the world—until the locket moved. She could not betray Ian, though he be dead a hundred years. Not this way. Her only purpose now was to stop Danforth, and so she lied, saying, "Yes, Edward, I did." She met his eyes, returning look for look.

The duke's face was blank as he got up. He bowed very formally to her. "Then I bid you good night, madam. May you and your Ian have joy this evening!" He left.

She waited until the door was shut and then found relief in tears, crying into the pillow so that she could not be heard. When she could cry no more, she softly talked to him, explaining (for it was important that he know) that it was *he* she wanted and no one else. It was he. Later, when most of her emotion had been spent, she tried to think. Her thoughts were not pleasant.

First she had tried to help her young cousin and failed. Then she had remained in what could only be called a depraved situation, closeted with a known whoremaster, and had enjoyed it! She had reveled in the attentions of a man known throughout the land for his immoral connections. She had luxuriated in what she had called friendship with one who only consorted with libertines and trollops. Happily wearing clothes bought for his whore, she had deluded herself that there was respect between them. And why? Nothing in her upbringing, in her whole life, could have sanctioned these last few days here!

From nowhere a thought appeared. She had, like any little fool, like the stupid woman that she was, she had fallen in love with him! To have fallen in love because of pleasing conversation, good manners, handsome looks, because of kindness toward her, because they had read many of the same books and held many similar opinions—what drivel! Men of his sort took mistresses, not wives.

That had been illustrated this evening. She had wanted him to make love to her, and was still bemoaning that she couldn't let him. Oh, she had allowed herself to behave like a common, besotted slut.

To be in love, but discover it a terrible thing— was there no wisdom in a woman? Gradually the sound she had been hearing all evening made sense. It was the dripping of eaves. The thaw had come.

She got up and went to the window, pulling open the curtains. In the moonlight she could see the rain, could watch the snow melt before her eyes. Evidently it had been thawing for some time, for there had been quite a runoff. Although the lane would be onerous, it would be possible to get through. Even if it were not, she would leave. She tried to calculate how much time had lapsed since Danforth left her, for she had to retrieve her belongings from the wardrobe. It must have been a couple of hours; he would be asleep.

Taking up a candle and shielding it with one hand, she tiptoed into the dressing room. There were snores from the other side of the room. She opened one of the large wardrobe doors, and put the candle down behind it so that the light would be hidden. Very quietly she took out her boots, cape, dress, and undergarments and brought them back into the bedroom. Yes, they were drab, undistinguished, ugly—but fitting for her. Widows should know their place and keep to it.

Elizabeth was relatively composed as she crept down the back stairway. She had to be out before the kitchen boy came down to light the fires. She unlocked the servants' door and stepped out. She was on the main road before daybreak.

Chapter Twelve

Awakened by a loud crashing noise, the duke sat up in bed before he realized that the sound came from the curtains being pulled open. He gave two "damnations," one for his valet for waking him and the other for himself. He had not had that much to drink the previous evening, or had he? As the rest of the night's events came back to him, he swore again. He would have to make that damnable woman an apology. Not that she did not owe him one too, using him, letting him make love to her and pretending he was her husband—that was beyond decency! Parker came to stand by the bed.

"Well, what is it?" his master demanded. "Why did you wake me? There had better be a damned good reason!" he warned.

"I beg your pardon, sir"—Parker's apology was perfunctory—"but as madam was not in her bed . . ."

"And you ran in to find her here? Doing it up too brown, Parker! How long have you been with me?" Danforth was more than irritated; this was beyond sense. "One moment, man—she is not in her bedroom?" The words finally had sunk in.

"No, sir," Parker answered, intently watching his master.

"Well, don't look at me that way. She isn't here! Besides, didn't I explain that she wasn't that kind of woman?" He wasn't sure why he felt protective of her reputation in front of this man, but he did.

"Yes, sir. And perhaps I should mention that I cannot find madam's own clothes in the wardrobe.

Polly also informs me that the kitchen boy found the back door unlocked this morning."

"God in heaven! Is the woman mad!" Danforth was having uphill work to absorb everything.

"The thaw has set in, sir. It appears that there might be a few places that would pose difficulties for a carriage, but that a person on foot would be able to get through." His master was not quick this morning, so he continued. "Was it not mentioned that madam had connections who lived further along this road? Perhaps she decided to visit them after all." He was gratified to note his master's frown as he turned to bring the duke his clothes.

Of course, Danforth thought, it would be just like her! He had done nothing but try to protect her reputation and yet she, without thinking further than that moment, had probably ruined herself. All impulse and then remorse later . . . Blasted woman!

As he dressed, he thought of further evidence of her birdwittedness, and it made him feel better. By the time he was being helped into his boots, he had sufficiently mellowed to make a suggestion. "Perhaps, if you could very tactfully discover if she is all right at the Buffords'. It is a mile on, I believe." Parker said he would see to it.

The duke ate his breakfast in front of the fire in the bedroom, and he was glad she was no longer any concern of his. If her cousins turned her out into the snow, it would serve her right. What story would she be able to give them to account for such an early arrival? He felt strangely lonely. It was female companionship that he missed, however, not her!

He felt at loose ends and went downstairs, where he got underfoot as the servants cleaned up the aftermath of last night's bacchanal. Lord Eversley appeared, and by the gingerly way he walked, it was not a good morning for him either. Benson was dispatched to the cellar for a bottle of brandy, and the two men went into the drawing room. They were slumped in their chairs in front of the fire, moodily watching the flames and holding their glasses when Parker entered.

"Well?" the duke asked without moving.

"Yes, sir. It was unsuccessful."

Danforth whirled around to confront the valet. "What do you mean, unsuccessful?" he demanded. "Why?"

"I could not say, sir."

"Hang it all, you two," Eversley said pettishly. "None of those confounded guessing games! Can't take them this early." He stared into his glass. "Can't take them at all!" he said decisively, and having made his judgment, returned to stare into the fire.

Both Danforth and Parker were accustomed to Lord Eversley, and they paid no attention to him. Danforth was irritated again. Dratted woman! It wasn't as if she were a maid either; she was a woman. To take such a pet because he had wanted her? She had refused him, but should that change their association? She was outspoken; she had disagreed with him before, had roundly told him off (another reason why he had enjoyed her). He felt betrayed. He had liked her.

Parker was waiting. "Better try the White Horse then," he said. Parker nodded and left, and the two men resumed their contemplations.

They were sitting in the same positions when Parker returned an hour later. Danforth was certain she was at the inn. He was trying to decide whether to confront her or just drive on to London—or perhaps visit one of his estates. There must be something he would like to do, and he was peevishly trying to determine what it was.

This time when Parker reported that he had no news, it disquieted the duke. Damnable woman! She had little money, he knew. She also still had a touch of her cold. He was not her keeper, but she showed no sense! For all of her knowledge she was not a worldly woman. She was very likely to meet someone who would take advantage of her. Addlebrained woman that she was, she was sure to!

He made a couple of circuits around the room and then walked into the hall. Parker followed.

"I took the liberty of checking on the condition of the road to Leicester. It is passable," Parker said noncommittally.

"Damn it all, Parker! I suppose you expect me to rush off to Margate just to make certain she arrived safely. She has no claims on me!" He glared at his man, daring him to say differently.

"I know that, sir."

"And it is not my fault she is bounding all over the countryside!" But his more honest self said that it probably was his fault—or at least partly. He gave up. "All right. Have it your way. Pack up. I suppose I might as well go to Margate as any other, but don't expect me to see her. You'll have to do it!"

Within the hour the duke had made his farewells and was on his way south.

Chapter Thirteen

The road was not as difficult as Elizabeth had expected. There were several low areas that seemed to
be ponds, and once she almost fell facedown into a
fast-moving rivulet, saving herself by quickly grab-
bing a low hawthorn branch, but she reached the
White Horse. The inn was filled with travelers, nois-
ily arriving and departing, all taking advantage of
the change in the weather. Elizabeth retrieved her
bag and penned a note to her cousin, begging her
to think again of the consequences; a coin in the
hand of the yard boy insured its delivery. She was
offered a ride into Melton Mowbray by a farmer who
was delivering his cheeses, and he in turn found
another farmer who was going into Leicester. The
roads were heavily trafficked and muddy, but the rain
had stopped. She arrived in Leicester with an hour
to spare before the York-to-London stage arrived.

She would not return to Margate. Whether it
seemed too tame after her misadventure or because
it was her heart that needed care, not her body, she
did not know. Elizabeth had been trying to think of
alternatives since leaving the White Horse, but not
until she was sitting in front of the fire at the stage
inn in Leicester, drying and warming her feet and
eating a large wedge of meat pie, did she think of
the Hendrickses. Charles and Melinda had been their
closest friends and Lindy had begged her to come
to them when Charles sold out six months ago, but
Elizabeth had declined. Why had she not thought
of them before; she would find a refuge there.

The further south the stage went, the kinder the

weather became, until it was hard for Elizabeth to remember the snow. She had probably been in the only corner of England where she could have been snowed in. *Satis superque.* She would not think of what could not be.

Elizabeth soon found her attention caught by the conversation of her fellow passengers, especially that of the fat lady in the corner, the possessor of a large family whom she made known to all. Elizabeth was wickedly amused at the story of the husband's gaffer, who had called the family together to announce he would die at noon on Lady's Day, and did, loudly cursing them all. After the old man's funeral eats, the clerk across from her began to hold forth on the notables he had seen, starting when he was but six. The fat lady recovered her breath and the conversation by telling of her sister-in-law's cousin's friend's account of once having seen the Prince Regent (or someone remarkably like him) enter his carriage. Her stories continued, one after another, until they reached London.

Elizabeth was not as lucky on connection as she had been northbound, for upon arriving in London, she discovered that the next stage to Canterbury did not leave until the following morning. She bought her ticket and went to find the quiet, reasonably priced inn which the clerk had recommended. She found it neither inexpensive nor quiet, but the sheets were clean and the street noises tapered off around two, letting her catch some sleep.

The following morning Elizabeth and four others boarded the stage. As the other passengers kept to themselves, Elizabeth's only distraction from her thoughts was to watch the trees and cottages pass by. Though the journey seemed interminable, they arrived in Canterbury in the early afternoon. Several of the hostlers suggested Elizabeth try the cattle market if she wanted sure transport to Ashford, so ignoring the great cathedral with its pilgrims, the medieval houses, the Roman ruins, and even the modern shops with their filled windows, Elizabeth made her way to the market. The information was correct; the third person she approached was ready to leave for Ashford. He carried her the twelve miles to the crossroads leading to Greenfields and waved her down the southwest road. Nothing untoward happened on the short walk—no snow, carriage, or churlish strangers—and within twenty minutes Elizabeth turned up the drive to Greenfields.

It was a short walk up to the early Georgian mansion surrounded on three sides by old maples and elms. The red bricks had softly weathered in the ninety-odd years since its erection, making it appear comfortable and welcoming. So jubilant was her reception by Charles and Melinda that Elizaeth cried —as did Melinda. They showed no surprise that she arrived unannounced; she was there, the long-awaited guest.

Melinda sent a maid up to light the fire in the best guest chamber and when she thought it was ready, bundled Elizabeth up the stairs to her room. Mrs. Frenshaw (Fretty), Melinda's maid-dresser, came in to greet Mrs. Elizabeth and take charge. She was glad to see her again; it was more than time Mrs. Beth came to them, and she would thank her mistress to go back downstairs so that she could get on with what needed to be done. Elizabeth promised to be quick, and Melinda kissed her again and left. Hot water was brought up, but Fretty insisted on getting a gown from Melinda's wardrobe, the one in Elizabeth's bag being too crumpled and undistinguished to be worn.

Elizabeth found her friends waiting for her in the green room, the small comfortable family sitting room. She stood in the doorway, happily returning their greetings. How good it was to be with them again. How could she have stayed away so long? Dear Charles had not changed, tall and erect with his red hair and military moustaches. Oh, perhaps there were five more pounds on his lean frame, but it was to his advantage. And Melinda—no, there was a difference. She was still the pretty, vivacious woman, but how fashionably dressed in the long-sleeved brown challis frock. And her dark hair was modish, short now. How very, very good to be with them!

There was so much catching up to do, friends who must be found, gossip to share, and telling each other how good it was to be together again, that it was a long time before there was a pause, and that was quickly filled by Melinda.

"And why, dear Beth, have you not congratulated the new earl?" she asked.

"I thought I had, or no, perhaps I hadn't. Oh dear ones, there is so much to say, I am not sure of anything." Elizabeth smiled at them both. "But how did it happen? You were Captain Charles when we last met. And your letter, Lindy," she said turning to her hostess, "was not a model of clarity."

Before Melinda could defend both her letter-writing ability and her notorious handwriting, Charles explained. "Did you remember that my grandfather on my father's side and the old earl were brothers? Well, his son had been dead for over twenty years, but there were two grandsons to carry on. Then Vivian was killed on the Bath road, and two months later John complained of indigestion and died that night. There I was, the Honorable Charles, and before we really were used to that, the old earl died, so here sitting before you, the fifth Earl of Hanthorne and his countess! It was even more of a shock to the rest of the family, for everyone had assumed I'd be killed in Spain. Shows you, don't it?" He grinned impudently at the ladies.

Elizabeth laughed and congratulated them.

"Oh, we're becoming ever so fashionable, Beth," Melinda announced grandly. Then she became serious. "No, but what is fun is suddenly having all of the money that we've always wanted. Not that we ever needed a penny more than we had," she hastily added, "but it is exciting to be able to buy whatever takes the fancy without thinking that mayhap there won't be enough to give to the cook for dinner tomorrow.

"And it's not all perfect, for we'll have to leave Greenfields and take up residence at the earl's seat, for there are so many things there that Charles has to attend to. But first we're going to London for at least part of the season. And dear Charles has promised that we can always come back here when we need to be not so grand." She found her husband's hand and held it.

Melinda had caught the quick expression on Elizabeth's face, and she suggested that they wait dinner no longer so that Elizabeth might retire early. "There will be time for everything, dear Beth, for now that you are here with us, we are determined that you stay awhile!"

Charles raised Elizabeth to her feet and stood holding her hands. "My dear Elizabeth, you cannot expect us to be unselfish. We will tolerate nothing but compliance, for you have delivered yourself into our hands." He kissed her cheeks, and Elizabeth felt her tears coming again as she returned his kisses and then was embraced by Melinda, who held her closely. They went into the dining room arm in arm.

Elizabeth slept until the following afternoon and her first thought upon waking was that she had overslept and kept Edward waiting. Tears came as she remembered where she was, but she made herself recognize her good fortune in having friends as dear as Charles and Lindy. She was not a child and first in love; she was a woman, old enough to know what life was really like. In a while she would be content again.

As she dressed herself in one of Melinda's day gowns, a soft cassinette with puff sleeves, she continued to talk sensibly to herself. One of the first things she must do was to send for her own clothes from Margate, although they were not so pretty or as fashionable as Lindy's. Her purse was thin too, and she would have to write Mr. Browlaw. For a woman determined to be independent, she had been living off all and sundry and must do so no more.

Melinda had been waiting for her to come down. "Charles said to let you sleep," she said as she kissed her, "so I had cook save lunch for you." She took Elizabeth's hand to lead her to the dining room. "Charles is closeted with his man of business so we can have a nice chat ourselves."

As soon as Elizabeth had been served, Melinda said, "Yesterday we talked of friends and of us, and since Charles is such a gentleman he would never dream of asking, but you know I am not so reticent, Beth, and I'm bound that something has happened." Elizabeth put her forkful of cold chicken down and looked at her. "Oh, don't look at me like that," Melinda ordered. "I smell something. I'll warrant there is a man involved!" She laughed as Elizabeth's eyes widened. "I knew it!" She said happily. "Now we shall wait until you are through, and we'll go off and have a cozy talk." She began to talk of other things.

Elizabeth's mind was confusion. She had not thought herself so transparent, or had Lindy only been guessing? Melinda talked about everything except the subject uppermost in both their minds, and as soon as Elizabeth's fork went down for the last time, she suggested they sit in the green room. Elizabeth wiped her mouth and smiled bleakly at her. "Has anyone recently told you that you are a nosy parker, love?" she asked.

"Heavens, yes, all of the time," Melinda answered, laughing. "Now come and we shall talk." But as they walked down the hall, she could not resist adding, "You do make a lovely widow, but you'd make an even more beautiful wife, so do tell me all—but not right now, for James is coming," and she opened the door and led Elizabeth to the divan across from the fire.

"I want to be able to see your face, Beth. Come, my dear, sit down and do tell Auntie Lindy all!"

Elizabeth sat down and tried to explain. "Lindy, I do love you, but there are some things that I can not talk about."

"Oh, nonsense!" retorted Melinda. "You aren't such a goose to think you are being disloyal to Ian by having fallen in love, are you?" She peered into her friend's face. "You both had such a lovely marriage, as good as Charles and I have," she added smugly, "but you must face facts. Ian is dead, and you are alive—and I want to know *all* about it." Elizabeth looked down at her hands. "You might as well tell me now, for you know I will get it out of you sooner or later." She waited.

Elizabeth looked up. "Lindy," she began, "it really

is not at all what you think." Melinda's face showed her disbelief. "No, I did develop a fondness for . . . but . . ." She sighed and looked away.

"Beth Campbell, what is the riddle?" Melinda demanded. "You weren't so nonsensical as to choose someone married, were you?"

"Oh, no," Elizabeth answered, horrified.

"Well, then—is he dreadfully poor? He's not one of those antiquated widowers taking the cure is he? Or . . ." She paused as she tried to think of what else might make her friend's selection unsuitable.

"Lindy, will you stop using your imagination?" Elizabeth said, laughing, for her friend's mind seemed infinite. It would be a relief to share it all with her, but not the wisest course, she decided, for there were things that not even Melinda could understand. "He is a rake, Lindy, a libertine," she said quietly.

Melinda was incredulous. "Now, you're funning me, Elizabeth! There is no way that you might even see such a man in that provincial retreat of yours! Was he hiding from creditors?"

"No, he is very rich, my dear."

"Rich, and a rake, and you met him! What have you been up to, Elizabeth? I vow you never met him in Margate!"

Elizabeth was startled. Melinda was too fortunate in her guesses. "Lindy, as I love you, this is not something that I can share. He is not aware that I care for him, nor did he try to engage my affections. It is not something that bears dwelling on. Dearest friend, I have done no more than be sorry for myself these last two years! I need to have a purpose, and I count on you and Charles to help me in my decisions." Elizabeth's voice was firm.

"Good! Then the first one will be that you come up to London with us for the rest of the season."

Elizabeth shook her head and Melinda took her hands, saying sternly, "Beth, you need to meet people—eligible suitors. Not your old fuddy-duddies, or even your rakes! You are a beautiful woman, yes, you are, and the sooner you get a decent wardrobe the better, for may I tell you that the gown you arrived in yesterday was beyond words!"

Elizabeth admitted she could use some gayer things, but not because she was looking for another husband. "I do care how I look now, but not to snare someone, for remarriage is not my goal! My fulfillment shall come from helping others."

Before Melinda could give Elizabeth her opinion, Charles came in. After their greetings, Melinda told him they needed the carriage the next day, for there was so much they had to do that it was a pity they could not start this very night. The conversation turned to cassimeres and grosgrains and surahs, until Charles protested and they discussed the news of the day until Melinda forgot and started on the shopping again.

While they were undressing for bed, Melinda told Charles about Elizabeth and of her insistence on finding some charitable works. He heard her out before speaking. "I can see, love, that a woman like Beth must have a purpose in life. I don't know why you are so opposed. It wouldn't suit you, nor many, but if she don't care to marry again, she must do something!"

"Oh, you ninny," his wife said affectionately, "can't you see the only reason she thinks that is because she's been hurt again? And besides, if she has given up all men, why is she interested in clothes, for you can do good deeds in anything, you know!" And since she had the last word, she pulled his moustache gently and kissed him. "Now, do go along with me,

Charles dearest. Good works be damned—it's good men we want!"

The next week was devoted to shopping, ordering clothes, and having fittings, Elizabeth borrowing a sum from Charles until her draft arrived. The ladies drove into Canterbury to look through several emporiums, finishing up in Ashford where the dressmaker lived. Elizabeth thought the selection too large, but with Melinda's help, she bought some blue sarcenet, two lengths of soft wool, six yards of sateen for an ordinary day frock, some crepon for a walking dress, material for a riding habit, and some colored satin for petticoats. She would not buy more than one pair of white kid gloves and a pair of silk stockings, contenting herself with six pair of cotton. A small dark blue beaver bonnet, two pair of satin slippers, and one pair of soft leather shoes with the rounded toes were finally ordered, but she said "no" to the sealskin muff. Lindy did agree it was dreadfully expensive and said she would loan Beth hers whenever it was wanted. Laces, bindings, handkerchiefs, reticules, and fans all had to be looked at too. Elizabeth was exhausted when she fell into bed each evening, which is what her hostess planned, and if she still cried, it could not be for long.

Chapter Fourteen

Melinda had definite plans for her friend, which did not include a lifetime of Christian benevolence—at least alone. She had kept Elizabeth busy the past week; for the coming one she concluded that a small dinner would be the thing. While they were all having breakfast in the small breakfast room, she announced her intentions. "I do think we all have been indolent long enough, my dears." Charles and Elizabeth exchanged amused glances, which Melinda ignored. "What I have in mind is that we have obligations that we have put off much too long, owing to the old earl's death and all, but now it is past time that we may entertain, and I'm sure that some of them have noted it."

Elizabeth was apprehensive at the thought, but when she tried to speak of her fears, Melinda would not listen. "Don't be fustian, Beth! It is not to be a dancing party, just a quiet dinner for some of our neighbors. I think a week from today would be a good time, and I shall need your help, for your handwriting is better than mine and you may do the invitations. The Trowbridges are interested in the Orphan's School in Canterbury, so you see your resolutions will be served." That settled, she turned to her husband. "And you, dearest, need to take care of the wines and all of that." She smiled at them both, and having assigned her tasks, she began to eat her breakfast.

After breakfast Elizabeth was placed at the small writing table in the green room and given a list of names. That the list numbered thirty-two did not unduly surprise her; Melinda enjoyed entertaining and would not think it a large crowd. Because she did not look out of the terrace windows often, she finished in three hours, and the footmen were given the cards and sent off to deliver them.

It seemed as if the whole estate were involved in the preparations for the dinner. The housekeeper, who kept everything spotless, insisted that the rooms be turned out again and the girls were brought in to help. The butler had to have the tableware counted, the silver shined, and more men to serve and so on, so three were added to his staff. The kitchen had to start on its sauces and sweets, cook and Melinda had to plan a menu, change it, and change it again, and two more helpers were needed. Even the stables had to make room for the guests' horses and brought some of the lads in to help. In between everything the ladies had to drive into Ashford for fittings. Melinda was exuberantly overseeing all, and again Elizabeth had little time to think as she tried to help her friend.

The day before the dinner Charles had to go into Ashford on business. He finished by three and, rather than return immediately to the maelstrom, he rode to the Boar's Tooth, an old inn at one of the side streets patronized by farmers and old country families. As he pushed his way into the large common room, he heard his name called. Looking around, he discovered a fashionably dressed gentleman standing and waving at him from a table near the fire. It was Lord Eversley, and seated with him was another gentleman, obviously also a member of the *ton*. Though unexpected, Eversley was always a most welcome companion, and Charles was smiling as he walked over to them. "What are you doing here, Eversley?" he asked.

Ignoring the question, Eversley called for a round and presented him to the Duke of Danforth. Waving Charles into a seat, he said, "Wanted something different. Looking over Danforth's estate. Very different, you know." Charles raised his brows, and Eversley quickly said, "No, I ain't rusticating! Just wanted something different."

"Richard, you would come after me," the duke said dryly.

"Oh, I know. But," he said, turning to Charles for support, "I ask you—Kent this time of year? No offense, Hanthorne, no offense." He brightened as three steaming mugs were set down on the oak table.

The duke turned to Charles. "Vivian Hendricks and I were good friends. I was sorry to hear of his death."

"Yes, Vivian was a right one," Charles replied. "Only person in the family I really knew."

"It was his regret that he could not go to Spain as you did. He held you in esteem."

"Wasn't to be thought of. The old earl was never in good health and someone had to look after things. But how Vivian would laugh now if he could see me trying to fill his shoes." They laughed and toasted their dead friend.

"What I want to know, Hanthorne, is why ain't you in London?" Eversley asked as their mugs went down.

"Oh, we'll be going up shortly. I still have some things to wind up here, and then we're off. I wasn't aware though," he said, turning to the duke, "that we were neighbors."

"We haven't always been. One of my mother's aunts

died without issue, leaving me Swatow Hall. Old Admiral Lord Langley's widow. You must have known her."

Charles had known the formidable relic, and Danforth shared some of the more libelous stories of the Admiral's career from cadet to the opening of the China trade. More time was spent catching up on their many mutual friends and acquaintances, until Charles looked at his watch and saw he was late.

"My wife will be sure I've fallen victim to a press gang," he said, rising. "I have an excellent proposal though. We are having a dinner tomorrow eve and would be honored if you both would join us."

They protested that his wife might not care to have her seating rearranged, but Charles was able to convince them that she was a right one and would be delighted. They accepted, and after giving them the time and directions, he left.

Charles rode fast, but as they kept country hours, it was half an hour past the dinner time when he arrived. Telling Evers he'd be down in ten, he ran upstairs to change. He knew his news would make up for his tardiness, but when he joined the ladies, he discovered they had a tale of their own.

Melinda hurried him into the dining room but let them be served before she announced, "Charles, you see before you a broken woman!" As she appeared her usual pretty self with every dark ringlet in place, he was not alarmed but sat waiting for her story.

"Do you know what has happened? Of course, you don't, but just do listen!" She paused to build up the suspense. "Cook has broken her leg! In two places, Dr. Grempfort says, and will have to be off it for at least six weeks, perhaps three months, and all because of mice." She took a sip of her wine.

"You know how everything is getting ready for our

dinner, well one of the scullery maids discovered mice in the preserve stores and she told the cook's boy to get rid of them. So he borrowed one of the groom's dogs (why not a cat, I'll never know), and when cook went to see what the terrible noise was and opened the door, some of the mice ran out and as she was standing in the doorway, they ran for her and the dog ran after them, but you know how fat cook is and she cannot move quickly and the dog became all tangled in her petticoats and down went cook—on the dog! Oh, Charles, you should have seen it! The groom is furious. He says the dog will never be the same!" They all laughed.

"Poor Beth and I dared not laugh, for everyone was so serious, and mad and all wanting to transport the cook's boy or at the very least, hang him. And it isn't good for cook either. But the terrible thing is, we have a dinner tomorrow night and cook is in bed!" She stopped to eat some turbot with ham sauce.

"Now, my charming husband, whatever should we do?" she asked. "Beth and I could stay in the kitchen and turn out a creditable meal, and Beth did offer, bless her, but I came up with just the thing!" She looked to Charles for approval. He smiled and she continued.

"Do you remember when Fretty's sister retired after being cook for thirty years to that very peculiar couple who used to travel all over the Continent? Well, she lives in Canterbury, just this side, and is bored. The footman took a note, and she will be here in the morning and delighted to be of service! Now, isn't that well done?" She happily accepted her due praise from her lord.

The rest of the evening was spent minutely detailing the disaster below, and Melinda was reminded that there was a message for Charles to please look in on the stables in the morning. Elizabeth then wanted to discuss her plans on decorating the hall with greenery and that led to reminiscences of other parties held there. It was not until Charles and Melinda were getting ready for bed that he was able to share his own news. Melinda chided him for keeping it back, but after a moment's reflection, said it might be for the best.

"For there is no getting over the fact, dearest, that Beth would not be happy if she knew two more gentlemen were coming—and pinks of the *ton* at that. Oh, Charles, that is such a coup!" She made a pirouette, smiling happily.

"No, dear, I think it well Beth does not know, for I do not want her upset. This will be exactly what she needs, but let us not mention it until needs be. I really do think you have done quite as well as I today." She gave her husband a thank-you kiss.

Charles received her thanks properly and enthusiastically, but after releasing her, he observed, "Lindy, I'm not so sure they are the answers to your prayers for Beth. They move in different circles, the *beau monde*. And they're not angling for wives; on the contrary Danforth's high steppers are the talk of the town—not that he'd trifle with a gentlewoman, mind you. No, I invited them because I enjoyed their company and I thought you would too. So keep that in mind, lady wife," he advised, "and don't go making plans that don't fit!"

Melinda smiled sweetly at her husband and changed the subject.

Chapter Fifteen

While Margate was renowned for the fine sands and fresh North Sea air, it was not frequented by the mode. Parker had procured a small guidebook for his master and suggested he might care to tour St. John's church, part of which dated back to the early twelfth century. The duke glared. Parker said he had thought his master wished himself to make inquiries and was only trying to make suggestions for what might amuse his Grace while he waited. The duke swore. After hearing once more that Mrs. Campbell had said she lived in the old section of town on a very small street and that the landlady's name was a bird, Parker said he would return by dinner and left.

As he'd walked through the hotel's public rooms, filled with invalids, gray beards, and unfashionables, the duke swore again. Because Parker had suggested the flint church, he perversely decided to walk on the pier, which was filled with invalids, gray beards, and unfashionables; and as he was healthy, well-dressed, and handsome, he attracted considerable interest, making him swear again. He went to the old church, but as it was worthy of interest, the churchyard was filled with the same unmentionables. He strode back to the main town, where he found a circulating library and borrowed last year's two volumes of *Self-Indulgence* and retreated to his room.

Their stay in Margate had followed this pattern: the duke remained in his room, having meals sent up and reading novels (which he made Parker find for him), while his valet searched the town. On the evening of the third day Parker returned late with the information that he had discovered a Mrs. Parrott on Lowbridge Street who had a lodger by the name of Elizabeth Campbell.

"Fancy you coming all this way and she ain't here now. She'll be sorry to have missed you!" Mrs. Parrott had said. "She don't have many visitors. No, she didn't leave notice where she'd be or when she'd be back. Just out of the blue she told me she had to be off, and off she went. She'll be back, for her things are here, but when there's no telling."

"Well, that's that," Danforth had said when he heard the report. "We'll leave first thing in the morning. How she ever expected to get well in a place like this, I'll never know. Damned depressing place!" He was satisfied he had done all he could to find her. His obligation was ended; there was no need to think of her again.

Danforth had told Eversley there were problems at one of his estates in Kent that required his attention, and with his business in Canterbury over, he had directed Hoare to Swatow Hall. The twenty-two miles were over good roads, and he arrived at his door before noon. He was descending from his coach as another coach pulled into his drive and his buoyant friend, Lord Eversley, shouted greeting.

The duke's departure from the hunting box had hastened the other guests, which hadn't bothered their host, for it had become a dead bore. There were no special functions in London to call him, and so he resolved to follow his hunch that something was up and visit Danforth in Kent.

His reception was cordial, if not effusive, and his chamber comfortable, if old-fashioned, for Lady Langley had spent the last years of her life driving to church or caring for three bad-tempered pugs. The house was in better condition than the farms, and Eversley accompanied his friend as he inspected the property. It was rather boring for him, and he was pleased to drive into Ashford, stopping at the Boar's Tooth before returning, where he found Hanthorne.

The duke had found Charles to his liking. Why it came to mind that Elizabeth's husband might have been such a man, when he was not even thinking of her, he could not say. The two friends spent the evening playing cards and idly gossiping. Both independently resolved to return to London the morning after Hanthorne's dinner.

Chapter Sixteen

Each of the upper servants looked out and pronounced it a magnificent day for her ladyship's dinner. Not a cloud was in sight and there would be a moon this evening so that the guests might stay as late as they wished. This good news was passed through the staff, and to their employers and guest, as final preparations got under way.

Elizabeth was in charge of decorating the hall with Evers and his staff at her disposal. When Charles's maternal grandfather built the house, instead of a large drawing room, he had a replica of a Tudor great hall built. When the house came to Charles's father, he painted all of the woodwork white, only leaving the great oak beams as they were, and it became a warmer, lighter room. He did not touch the huge fireplaces at each end but did convert the lower windows into bays with seats in them. Large portraits of various family members in ornate gilded frames, each indicative of the era in which it was painted, lined the walls, with room for only two mountain scenes, one of the Highlands and the other of Switzerland. An assortment of marble busts was scattered in and about the massive tables and chairs.

Elizabeth vowed it would look festive when she was done. She covered the alcoves with greens, transforming them into bowers, and then went to the fireplaces. Each had a chimney glass in a gilded frame over it, and with her same footman helper, she hung greens over the frames and mantels. While she was doing that, the others under Evers's supervision took the long strands woven from evergreens by the gardeners, and suspended them from the beams. Feeling impish, Elizabeth fashioned garlands for each of the busts, an improvement of sorts, she felt. She stood back in the doorway as the servants finished the ceiling. With the greens and the candles lit all around the walls, including those of the brass floor candle holders, it was doubtful if anyone would notice that the brown damask curtains were fading.

At their late lunch Melinda had a touch of last-minute panic. Why had she not planned for music; dancing after dinner would have been so nice. Charles reminded her she'd wanted a quiet dinner and that it was their first party since the old earl's death. Elizabeth added that she would have been unlikely to find musicians to her standard at such short notice. Melinda was mollified and her usual good humor returned as they discussed the dinner to come. She suggested that the ladies rest as they wanted to look their best. Elizabeth agreed. Her back ached from reaching above her head, and she wanted to remove the pine needles that had fallen down her shift.

Elizabeth was tired but was looking forward to the evening, for it was impossible not to catch Melinda's excitement. She could not imagine why she had not come to Greenfields sooner. How strange to realize it was barely three weeks since she had left Margate— and the duke again intruded into her reflections. She picked up a book of poetry that Melinda had loaned her and made herself read of gentle sheep and cows in meadows mild until she fell asleep.

There had been long discussions on what to wear before the final selections were made, and then as the ladies dressed, there were last-minute qualms and changes. Melinda had chosen a yellow satin tunic dress caught in at the high waist and falling straight down over the narrow skirt ending just above golden satin slippers. Her short hair was brushed and curled so that when Fretty wound the deep yellow turban over it, the curls showed. She picked up and discarded several necklaces until she tried Charles's mother's amber. It was a double strand that came down to her low neckline and when she added the long drop earrings and looked in her mirror, the rich golden beads reflected the lights, and she was satisfied. On her left wrist, over long white kid gloves, she put two gold bracelets, and on her right, one of gold and one of ivory. When she went downstairs, she would carry her Spanish fan.

Elizabeth wore one of her new dresses: a short-waisted blue sarcenet frock with a becomingly low décolletage. Blue satin slippers covered her new silk stockings, and she danced a few steps, feeling deliciously extravagant. Fretty came in to dress her hair in the Roman style, piling it on top of her head, curling it softly in front, and letting the back fall down her neck. A tiny white lace wisp of a cap was secured on the top of her golden hair. She looked grand, but Fretty told her not to wiggle so much. She fastened her pearls around her neck, pulled the long white kid gloves up over her elbows, and was ready to go to Melinda's room.

Elizabeth's own pearls were too short, Melinda said as she took them off and put her own long rope around her friend's neck. The pearl cluster earrings had to be worn too, and when Elizabeth saw herself in the glass, she had to agree they softly complemented her gown. She smiled her thanks, for Melinda would not let her say anything.

She declined the loan of several bracelets and did not care to redden her cheeks. Charles called to them, and taking one last look at themselves in Melinda's full-length mirror, they went to parade before him in the hallway.

Charles was all admiration. "You're a fine collection of womanhood, my lovelies!" he said, and he kissed his wife's cheek. "I'm glad I have my ring on you, my lady! And you, Beth, you are very taking this evening. You do us proud!" He kissed her too.

They happily accepted his compliments and then told him how well turned out he was in his light green coat and fawn knee breeches. "You were handsome in your uniform, dear Charles, but you are splendid now!" Melinda said. Still smiling, the three passed down the main stair and through the passage to the hall, where they would receive their guests.

Chapter Seventeen

Melinda told Elizabeth they would not have long to wait. "Country people are not like those in London," she said, where they come as late as they can to show their consequence. Our guests will be most punctual." Only twenty minutes later Evers announced the first guests. Elizabeth tried to be calm.

Charles and Melinda were universally liked and everyone was delighted to make the acquaintance of their friend. Elizabeth gave up trying to remember names but continued to smile as she was introduced. Dr. Grempfort greeted her as an old friend and inquired about his patient, so the mice story had to be repeated to those nearby, and Elizabeth found herself talking and laughing as if she had always known them. There were several retired officers among the guests; they and their wives were especially welcomed.

When all but two or three of the guests had arrived, Melinda took Elizabeth over to one of the groups and, when an animated conversation started about the proper use of grappling hooks in siege warfare, Melinda quietly left them. Sir Edmund Northingfrade and Colonel Warrington each had particular views. Elizabeth's back was to the door and Colonel Warrington's parade-ground whisper drowned out Evers's announcement of the last two guests.

The duke of Danforth and Lord Eversley stood in the doorway looking for their hosts. Neither could fail to notice Elizabeth; she was a striking woman in the group of older men and women near them.

Eversley's spirits picked up, and he drew his shoulders even straighter, while Danforth felt as if he had taken a blow to the middle from Cribb himself.

To his hosts the duke appeared unruffled as he drawled his apologies for their tardy arrival, but his lips were grim as he bowed and kissed Melinda's hand. Charles took them to meet Elizabeth, who had just asked Sir Edmund if he meant the siege of Acre or Constantinople. She turned in answer to Charles's hand on her arm to find herself confronted by Danforth. Elizabeth could not move or speak; the blood rushed out of her body. Charles made the introductions, and when Elizabeth did not respond, he turned to find her on the point of fainting.

"Here now, Beth, come sit down!" he said, reaching for her.

"Allow me, Hanthorne," the duke's hand went to her arm, and before anyone else could move, he was taking her away from the guests and toward one of the window alcoves. "Get hold of yourself, my dear Mrs. Campbell," he said coldly as he seated her, "unless you want to provide more speculation about yourself than you already have." He remained towering over her.

Charles completed the introductions to Lord Eversley and then excused himself, saying that Mrs. Campbell had been in seclusion since the death of her husband two years before, and he hoped the evening would not prove too tiring for her. He went for Melinda, trusting that whatever had gotten to Elizabeth, his wife would be able to deal with it.

Melinda, who had seen the duke and Elizabeth walk to the window seat, was making her way to Charles to ask him about it; this was not wise of Elizabeth. Charles took her aside.

"A moment, Lindy. Beth almost swooned, and Danforth took her away to collect herself."

"Swooned! Good God, why?"

"I don't know, but something has to be done before it is generally noticed."

"Do not worry, Charles; I'll take care of this. Do mingle with our other guests." Melinda regretted that she had left the vinaigrette in her room.

"Well, my dear, what is the matter?" she asked as she came up to the couple.

Elizabeth had been trying to calm herself. She was lightheaded no longer, but she was very afraid she was going to cry. Danforth, so angry he could not speak, continued to silently loom over her, but he came to her rescue without thinking.

"I am sorry, but it was my fault, Lady Hanthorne. Mrs. Campbell's husband and I were close at one time, and the shock of seeing me again brought back memories that were painful for her."

Elizabeth quickly looked up, but his face was impassive and he did not look at her. "I do think she will be recovered in a few minutes, ma'am. My apologies, Mrs. Campbell." He bowed and walked away.

Their eyes followed him as he joined a group at the far end of the room. Elizabeth made herself speak. "Lindy, I am sorry." Could she leave the gathering? She longed for the privacy of her room.

Melinda sat next to her. "I may sound brutal, dearest Beth," she began, "but as Ian lived on this earth some thirty years, you will discover many things and people that will remind you of him. Come now, you have resolved to go forward; you must make yourself go on." She took one of Elizabeth's cold hands. "I did not know there was an acquaintance between the duke and Ian. I would not have thought it, but then I know Charles found both him and his lordship congenial yesterday and thought we might too."

"Good, there is color in your cheeks now," she said, standing up and raising Elizabeth. "Now, I want to bring you to the Trowbridges; you will be interested in their project." Melinda continued to talk as she brought Elizabeth into the group and helped her enter into the conversation.

Lord Eversley made his way over to where Danforth was standing and as soon as he could, he spoke *sotto voce* to his friend. "Damned fine-looking woman. Why didn't you mention her? Didn't know you knew her husband."

The duke smiled grimly at his irrepressible friend. It would serve him right were he told she was his houseguest less than a fortnight ago! "I knew Campbell when he was in London several years ago. He was much like our host; you would have liked him. As for his widow," he paused for a moment, then said, "she's passable, yes, but not my style," and he turned to the younger gentleman on his left, who announced he rode with the Cottesmore.

Eversley looked back to where Elizabeth was. Although she was not as animated as when they had first seen her, she certainly was more than just passable. There might be something for country living after all, he thought, and he began to saunter in her direction as dinner was announced.

Earlier Elizabeth had protested that she did not want to be the guest of honor. All would know she was a guest at Greenfields; to be introduced as their friend was sufficient. Charles resolved the matter by pointing out that she would be more comfortable seated on his right with a stranger on her other hand than sitting through dinner between two unknowns. And so when dinner was announced, Elizabeth went out on Charles's arm.

Chapter Eighteen

Melinda and Evers had transformed the coldly formal dining room into a brightly festive chamber. All of the oil lamps were lit: along the walls, on the sideboards, and in the chandeliers; and on the table the long tapers burned in the four silver candelabras made in the form of cupids cavorting in a glade, a gift to Charles's grandfather by a grateful Frederick II. The light caught and sparkled in the cut-glass goblets and wine glasses, in the silver serving dishes, and even in the queen's pattern silverware. It was brightly reflected from the high-polished mahogany sideboards and glowed softly on the wainscoting.

The large folding doors had been pulled open to make the dining and smaller breakfast room into one. More sections were added to the mahogany table to seat the thirty guests, there having been four regrets. Melinda's mother's soft paste porcelain dishes were set on the white damask cloth. It might not be the Pavilion, but Elizabeth forgot her own distress for the moment as she felt proud for Charles and Melinda. The room was as warmly welcoming as their hearts.

The Duke as highest-ranking guest was on his hostess's right. Their first attempts at conversation were not very successful. Why dear Charles had thought him particularly agreeable, Melinda could not understand. Danforth was aloofly correct; his mind was occupied with Elizabeth and his plans for her once he could get her alone. No other woman in his thirty-six years had infuriated him as much as she! He found his hostess a prattling fool.

"—Charles's best friend so Beth and I became good friends too. I am so pleased that you knew him. Was he not a superior man? And what a good dear friend —such grand times we four enjoyed together. *Requiescat in pace,* Ian." Melinda sighed. "But you were not acquainted with Mrs. Campbell, I believe?"

She now had his full attention, accompanied with his very sincere wishes for the Major's repose. "No," Danforth answered, "I met Campbell before they were married, but we shared a few good evenings and I daresay he must have mentioned my name to her. I trust she will be all right."

There had been nothing in his words to give offense, but there was something in his manner that made Melinda's eyes narrow. "Of course, Mrs. Campbell is all right. She has more mettle than many of the gentlemen here!" Her voice was tart, but her smile was gracious.

Turning to her left, she began to ask Mr. Fisher about the dreadful assassination of last May, for Mr. Fisher was an M.P. and had been in the House of Commons when Perceval was shot. Melinda had not had the opportunity of asking him about it before, and she was filled with questions.

Danforth was claimed by Lady Warmner who wanted to discuss the Princess Charlotte, a topic much debated throughout the kingdom, for she was the Prince Regent's only child.

At the far end of the table Elizabeth was almost relaxed under Charles's protection. She avoided looking in the duke's direction, trying to put, and keep, him out of her mind. The only reference Charles had made to the incident in the hall had been to softly ask *"estas bien?"* and, at her nod that all was well, he began to talk about the Prince of Orange. Charles had been asked if he had met the possible suitor to the Princess Charlotte. He had, for the prince was now serving as one of Wellington's aides-de-camp. They speculated on whether the princess would like him, and if not, then who might be under consideration.

On her right was Lord Warmner, a stout man toward the end of his middle years, who was pleased to find himself next to Elizabeth. He kindly asked if she were enjoying her stay in Kent. His favorite estate was the one near Maidstone, and he was able to describe it to her. How it differed from other such establishments, Elizabeth did not discover; however he placed few conversational demands on her, requiring little more than her sympathetic ear.

Later he favored her with his views on the repeal of the Orders in Council. "Our nation's life is trade, madam, trade! To prohibit our exports was madness." Elizabeth discovered she was eating the fillets of mutton larded, roebuck fashion, which meant that either she had been eating for some while or the footmen had passed her by as they served. Charles turned to her with some comments about his new horse, and she surreptitiously inspected her plate. It certainly looked as if it were the rabbit à la chausseur on the upper right. Charles asked if anything were amiss, and she made an answer. Elizabeth knew the menu almost as well as Melinda; dinner must be almost over.

Charles was interested in ballooning. He had a friend who knew Sadler, and Charles thought he would look him up when they went to town. Lord Warmner extolled the virtues of country living and as Elizabeth was raised in Hampshire, the old Wessex of King Alfred, his lordship continued to regard her as a woman of superior understanding. Elizabeth had never greeted Naples biscuits with such pleasure, they not being favorites of hers, but their presence indicated that the last course had been served. It must have been a successful dinner, but Elizabeth could not have vouched for it.

Melinda gave the signal for the ladies to rise and, as she passed her husband, again reminded him not to let the gentlemen linger too long. Charles smiled and promised.

The ladies had time to talk of comfortable things, and Melinda was roundly congratulated on the presence of the two nonpareils, Danforth and Eversley. Mrs. Trowbridge brought Mrs. Hubert Creighdon, a woman noted for her efforts on behalf of maimed and indigent soldiers, and presented Elizabeth to her. Mrs. Creighdon was gracious. "Everyone says that something must be done for those poor unfortunates," she said, "but very few come to their aid. We need more serious-minded gentlewomen such as you, Mrs. Campbell." Elizabeth felt a hypocrite, for her mind was very far from humanitarian considerations at the moment. She accepted Mrs. Creighdon's invitation to visit her projects in Canterbury with a proper show of interest as the gentlemen rejoined them.

Chapter Nineteen

Elizabeth was listening to Mrs. Creighdon's recounting of the plight of a veteran who had served under Cornwallis in the Americas. She felt as if she were the hare watching the dogs come closer, as both the duke and Lord Eversley made their way toward her. Eversley reached her first and, as soon as Mrs. Creighdon finished, he bowed to them both and turning to Elizabeth said, "I do think I have a case against our host, Mrs. Campbell. You must tell me if I might call him out. As one of Charles's oldest friends, I do protest that we have not met before!"

Elizabeth quickly decided he was the lesser evil and forced herself to return his smile. A fuming Danforth had been seized by Mrs. Creighdon, who had been desirous of meeting him all evening. There was some property that she knew he owned in Canterbury which would be excellent for an extension of one of her Homes. She also was an intimate of his Aunt Sarah, and Danforth made himself be civil. She was obliging enough to summarize her plans for the unfortunate creatures.

While Mrs. Creighdon particularized her arrangements, he could hear Eversley being charming to Elizabeth and her pleasant responses to his fatuous remarks. Dark thoughts concerning strangulation for his lordship and either forcible abduction or public flogging of the strumpet filled his head. At last he disengaged himself from Mrs. Creighdon, but not before she extracted a promise to inspect one of her projects. "And Mrs. Campbell has promised to come too," she said.

Tea was served. Eversley was unintermittent in his attentions to Elizabeth, but each time Danforth freed himself from one conversation to join her, he was captured by another. Melinda had kept Eversley and her friend in view, smugly watching their continued association. As soon as she could, she joined them.

"I was just telling Mrs. Campbell how much I enjoy your charming Kentish countryside," Eversley said. "Your winters here are so much milder than those I've just been through in the north. In fact, I am inspired—would it not be agreeable to make a small expedition to see more of it?"

Melinda thought his lordship's proposal excellent. Elizabeth, whose stomach had tightened at the mention of the northern winter, was trying to discreetly locate Danforth, but at the moment he was hidden behind a foursome. She could not readily find him before she had to make an answer to Melinda, who had accepted an invitation for all of them, the following day but one, and called upon Elizabeth to second it.

George and Lydia Neivens, good friends of the Hanthornes, had joined the group and had offered to give a luncheon as well as arrange a tour of their old church. Lydia knew that Elizabeth would enjoy it. "We have an old Norman church that is very beautiful, Mrs. Campbell. Lindy has told us of your interest in such things. Fortunately it has escaped both embellishment and modernization, and our vicar's knowledge of the church is second to none."

"And if it is too cold to ride, we shall take the carriage," Melinda decided.

Lord Eversley promptly offered an alternative. "My dear Lady Hanthorne, Danforth and I shall come for you—if we may. His coach is all the latest crack and you would find it most comfortable." Melinda was happy to accept.

A light repast was served at eleven thirty in order that those who had far to travel might leave early. Danforth had given up on his attempts to reach Elizabeth, but she was careful to remain in large groups. Lord Eversley still kept to her side. Elizabeth had concluded that there was no harm in his lordship, even if he was making her his latest flirt. His manners were pleasing and his conversation amusing. She could understand why he was so well liked. That he had hosted such a house party had nothing to do with his treatment of her. No, she did not find him disturbing; if only the same were true of his friend!

On the ride back to Swatow Hall, Eversley was very cheerful; the evening among provincials had not been flat, after all. He enjoyed discussing Mrs. Campbell, and if he received few responses from his friend, he did not notice. The duke had an unaccustomed headache.

Elizabeth went up to bed with a headache too. She had kept herself together all evening, except for those first dreadful moments when she had been faced by Danforth, but by the time the last guest departed, her body ached. She kissed and thanked her friends, but begged to be excused and went to her room. Fretty came in to make sure the evening had not been too much for her, helped her undress, and tucked her in. Fretty returned a few minutes later with some balm tea, standing over Elizabeth until two cups were drunk, the tea being helpful to both body and soul. It worked, for just after she made the decision to return to Margate the next day, Elizabeth fell asleep.

Even after they were in bed, Charles and Melinda continued to review the evening.

"And dearest, after the *contretemps* with his Grace, I was sure the dinner was done for, but instead Lord Eversley was exceedingly attentive." Melinda smiled knowingly.

"One minute, my sweet," Charles protested. "Although Eversley was amicable, that doesn't mean you can start smelling orange blossoms!"

"Charles dear, no man knows that he is ready for marriage until he is properly caught!"

"No man?"

"Oh, but my love, you were ever different!" and she kissed him. "Now, as for your duke, what a boorish man he is! I can not see why he is such a catch —except that he does have money and rank. No, I do not find him congenial. I pity the poor female who marries him!"

Chapter Twenty

Danforth awoke with the same subject on his mind as when he went to sleep: how to speak privately with Elizabeth. He resolved to ride over to Greenfields as early as a morning call was permissible. Parker opened the curtains and asked what time they would be departing. It took a few seconds to remember that he had said they would leave this morning.

"I find that I have some small business with Lord Hanthorne," Danforth said, "and after that, we shall see."

"Very well, sir. Will Lord Eversley be waiting too?"

"Devil take Eversley! Ask him yourself."

"Very well, sir," and Parker left to inform the staff of the changes in plans before returning to help his master dress.

The duke selected his clothes carefully. If Parker thought it unusual that such pains were taken for a country visit, he kept silent. His Grace tried three coats before choosing a deep blue superfine double-breasted one with brass buttons. It went well with his striped waistcoat. Leather breeches and top boots completed his outfit. He looked ready for a ride through Hyde Park.

Having no taste for food, he went down for his horse, which was waiting at the front door. He was a black gelding purchased and sent down six months before when poor Treymont was breaking up his stables. The five miles to Greenfields were quickly covered, and he was turning into the drive as shouts came from behind him. He stopped and turned. Lord Eversley came riding up.

"Damn it all, Edward! I've tried to catch up with you the whole way!" he said as he came alongside. "Why didn't you tell me that you were coming over? Could have rode together."

"What in hell are you doing here, Richard?" The duke was in no mood for social amenities.

"Oh, forgot to mention it last night. Have to make plans, you know. Well, are we going to sit in the drive and talk?" he put his knees to his horse.

Danforth caught up with him. "No, I remember why I didn't say anything last night," Eversley said as they went up the drive. "You was in one of your black moods. Told me to snuff it." A thought struck him. "Why are you here so early? You ain't one to get up in the morning!"

"I need to see Hanthorne on business," Danforth answered gruffly. "What plans are you talking about?"

A young lad, who had been busy raking the last traces of last night's guests from the gravel, laid down his rake and ran up to take their horses. Eversley smiled at the boy, walked up to the door, and gave a good rap to the knocker.

"I'm here to see the ladies, Edward, so I won't interfere with your talk with Charles," Eversley said kindly. Evers answered the door and his lordship gave his name to take to Lady Hanthorne and the duke's for the master. Before Danforth could speak, Charles came into the hall. He was surprised to see the two gentlemen so early but took them into his office-library and asked Evers to bring a tray.

"Did your lady tell you about the day trip we planned last night?" Eversley asked. "Thought I'd better check one or two things with her before getting on with it. Edward here wants to speak to you on business."

Evers brought in a tray, three bottles, and two different kinds of glasses. In response to their nods Charles poured three glasses of brandy. He was grateful for Melinda's hints from last night; it helped explain Eversley's arrival. A bit of gallantry would be a good thing for Elizabeth. As for his Grace, Charles tried without success to think of any business they might have. The duke was trying to think of some too.

Melinda had almost finished dressing when the message was brought up that there was a caller. Fretty had a hard time making her sit still so that the last few ringlets were perfect. She looked in the mirror; the white wool dress was not by a London modiste but the lines were good. She was very excited for Elizabeth. Fretty said she would see to Mrs. Beth's hair.

Melinda went into Elizabeth's room to tell her of the visitors. Elizabeth was wearing her light blue sateen dress. It was one of her new ones, and she looked very handsome in it.

Melinda secretly wished Beth had chosen a more elegant gown, but she knew better than to make mention of it.

"So do come down as soon as you can. Fretty is coming to do your hair. His lordship is an amusing rattle; we all enjoyed him last night. The duke's come too. He wants to see Charles on some business. What that could be, I have no idea. Now do hurry, and don't worry." Melinda kissed her and swept out.

Elizabeth sat at her dressing table. Edward had come to see Charles on business? He had not come to see her? Not that she would consent to an interview, but he would not even try? She stared ahead, the mirror reflecting her unhappy eyes. She would go down because Lindy wanted her to. "Out of nothing, nothing comes." She must make arrangements to leave this very day.

Melinda fetched his lordship from Charles and brought him to the green room. It was easy to see why he was so popular with both sexes. There was a kindness in him as well as a sense of humor. He would be so very right for Elizabeth.

Charles and Danforth remained in the office, each one waiting for the other to speak. The duke was trying to bring his mind back from Eversley and his interest in Elizabeth. They would not suit.

"My dear Hanthorne," he slowly began, "my mind seems to be on a myriad of things this morning, and as you and your charming wife are the cause of one of them, I have come to you."

Charles tried to avoid appearing skeptical.

"Your Mrs. Hubert Creighdon is close to my Aunt Sarah, the Countess of Richmount, fondly called 'the terror of Richmount' by the family. Mrs. Creighdon is interested in some property that she thinks I own in Canterbury—I would not know. She was able to extract a promise from me that I go with her to see one of her projects and review the property in question." His voice became very casual. "She suggested that Mrs. Campbell would be interested too. It would be more enjoyable, if we all might go together. There is an inn that provides a good lunch, and I can reserve a room if it is agreeable."

Known for his good sense and kind heart, Charles was accustomed to being called upon by friends and acquaintances to offer advice and assistance. He knew when to speak and when to remain silent. Stubby Thompson came to Charles about his gambling debts before he dared speak to his own colonel. Even the reticent Don Alfred Miguel Jesús Antonio Martínez del Arroyo spent one dark night with Charles before leaving at dawn to return home and put the bullet between his eyes. Crossed in love, a question of honor, should land be ploughed or left fallow—all would benefit from Hanthorne's counsel.

Why then was the duke's request unexpected? Because Charles had pegged him as a very self-sufficient man, one who would not quake before a Mrs. Hubert Creighdon. His reputation was of a proud, reserved aristocrat; did he count Charles among his intimates? Moreover, this man before him now was not the same gentleman whom he had met and liked at the Boar's Tooth two days ago. Charles quickly had to determine which evaluation was correct, and he decided to trust his first instincts; the duke was basically sound, but for some unknown reason he now was under considerable tension.

"My dear Duke, of course you may count on me. I happen to know that Mrs. Campbell has a true interest in Mrs. Creighdon's schemes, and I am sure that she would want to come too. Mrs. Campbell needs to have something to do, and while I do not agree with her that remarriage is not to be considered, this sort of work is always beneficial." Charles was surprised with himself for revealing so much of Elizabeth to this man who barely knew her. The thought came that there might be something here, but he rejected it outright.

"Come, we'll join the ladies and Eversley and make it all definite. You are, I take it, accompanying the party tomorrow?" Charles rose to his feet, ready to bring his guest to the green room.

The duke found it difficult to return Hanthorne's smile, but he did. More than ever he wanted to see Elizabeth—but not in Richard's company, nor with anyone else. He was reacting as if he were a love-sick swain in a lady's romance, and as the significance of his thought struck him, he looked up at Charles in wonder.

He stared at Charles a good minute before he saw him. "Hanthorne," he said as he got up, "I am not usually such a fool. I apologize! No, my steward has requested an interview and I have one more call to make before I can return." He was calm now, almost himself. "I shall count on you and your lady—and of course, Mrs. Campbell—not to abandon me to Mrs. Creighdon. As to the outing tomorrow, I am not sure for—"

Charles interrupted him. "It is to be to the Neivens, whom you met last night. You look as if you could use a diversion. Their cellar is one of the best in Kent."

"Then I am delighted to go. My regrets to the ladies this morning, and my profound thanks to you. Until tomorrow, Hanthorne." He shook Charles's hand and left.

If the duke had found the ride to Greenfields disquieting, it was nothing to the return ride. He was in love! At his age too. He had no wish to be in love with Elizabeth—or anyone.

His life was pleasurable, his household well run, his estates well managed. But he was not happy, was he? Elizabeth was but a woman with whom he had shared some hours—many long, enjoyable hours, even days. They had spent more time together than most people did before they married. They had become well acquainted. Elizabeth had carried herself well in a very bad situation. She was no girl, but a woman —a lovely, enchanting woman, but also a frustrating, pigheaded shrew! But how he missed her. She had passion. Did she have sense? And what did he want in a wife? A woman who loved him, and no one else.

How much did she still care for her dead husband?

No, Elizabeth was no virginal, pliable chit, but a mature, beautiful woman. He was accustomed to women—he had had many—but he had never felt this way about any of them. He needed to talk to her, be alone with her. Danforth laughed aloud. He had been trying to talk to her for days! He continued to try to put his thoughts into order, but through it all, one remained stable—he wanted Elizabeth!

Chapter Twenty-one

Elizabeth joined Melinda and Lord Eversley in the green room. They had been discussing the Royal Family and after greeting Elizabeth, they continued. Melinda planned to take her proper place in London society and wanted up-to-the-minute information on everything so that she would not appear too green. Eversley was the perfect one to ask; he was *au courant* on the news of the street or of the Queen's Council.

They had begun on the King and Queen with expressions of admiration and affection for the poor, mad ruler and his patient consort. Eversley's father had known him when he was more or less himself; it must have been in 1800, for the king had slipped in and out of his madness since '02.

After the expressions of loyalty to their rulers, they began on the interesting parts of the family, the Royal Dukes, who were universally disliked, with the exception of Clarence. Clarence did as he pleased. Had Melinda heard the old story of when he was a sailor and had been ordered to go to the West Indies? He'd ignored his superior's orders and sailed into Plymouth instead. The King had been greatly startled.

Cumberland—Eversley would not discuss him. Even the Royal Family spoke of him in horror. Melinda was conversant with York and his problems and had met him once. Eversley was not going to mention Mary Anne Clarke, his greedy *demimondaine*, but Melinda brought up her name so they had a cozy chat about her.

Kent was a martinet. "The most hated man in the

army," Melinda avowed. Was Eversley aware that he had caused a mutiny in Gibraltar because of the severity of his discipline? Everyone knew that. As for Sussex, he was innocuous, a warmhearted fool.

On to Cambridge, who lived most of the year in Hanover; Melinda might not meet him. He was totally unlike the rest of the family. He lived with his own wife, within his means, and all of his children were legitimate.

Finally to the most interesting of all, His Royal Highness, the Prince of Wales. Melinda agreed not to talk about his wife or the bickering and hatred between the two. "I suppose she is to be pitied, but I cannot like her," she asserted. Eversley agreed but had to quote the latest from that quarter. Last month when there was all of the to-do about the Princess Charlotte and should she have another governess or a lady-in-waiting, her mother had written to Prinny objecting that her daughter was denied social intercourse with young ladies of her age. He would not answer for over a week and then it was to say that he had "not been pleased to express his pleasure thereon." Melinda clapped her hands.

Had they been in the country during the "Royal Sprain"? That must have occurred a year ago, for it was in the winter. There was a party given by the Duchess of York at Oatlands and while dancing with his daughter, the Princess Charlotte, Prinny had bumped into a chair or a sofa leg and hurt his foot. But when he left Oatlands, word went round that he had grossly insulted Lady Yarmouth and that her husband had thrashed him soundly!

As of last year Lady Jersey was out (although they were still friends); it was Lady Hertford now. She was forty-seven if she was a day, but still a Celebrated

Beauty. The Pavilion at Brighton was a fantastic sight and the Regent was constantly changing it. No wonder he was always in debt.

Elizabeth had to do nothing more than nod or murmur in the correct places. Eversley and Melinda were so engrossed in their own subject that they didn't notice her preoccupation. Elizabeth could dispassionately note Eversley's good looks and recognize his charm without being touched by it. There would be a few more years before he would care to settle down; but the man that she chose would have to be faithful to her, from the beginning to the ends of their lives!

That she had neither a man nor his love was emphasized when the door opened and only Charles entered. Her face fell and, though she recovered quickly, Charles caught it and came over. "What's wrong, Beth?" he quietly asked.

"Nothing that a good night's sleep won't mend, Charles dear." She was completely under control now as she smiled at him.

Melinda and Eversley looked up, and she gaily greeted her husband. "Why did you not bring Lord Eversley to us before, love? Do you know all of the marvelous things he knows? He has the nicest plans for tomorrow too. I'm really very excited!"

"My dear Lindy, we all can see that," Charles answered laughing. "As to why I kept Eversley hid— don't forget that I only sold out six months ago and Richard here is such a gadfly that no one knows when one will meet him next."

"No, Charles," Eversley said, "I add my protests to that of your lovely wife. I suspect you of deliberately hiding her so that I could not have the honor of telling her stories. And as for the delightful Mrs. Campbell, you positively have had her buried in a cave— or was that Merlin—but you do know what I meant!"

Again Charles had caught Elizabeth's wince, and he changed the subject. "Now, what are the nice plans, Richard? Shall we go in costume? Or by river barge? Though I warn you, it will be difficult as we are unconnected by even the merest trickle of water."

"You are just jealous of my organizational talents. I am worthy of Frederick the Great! Naturally we shall go by Danforth's coach."

"And, Charles, he has one of those lovely new ones with many springs and so much room inside; it will be just the thing. In fact, although I suspect they are shockingly expensive, we must get one when we get to London, for the one we have must have been bought for the old King's coronation!"

They fell into easy bantering and, with Charles present, Elizabeth had to participate. Finally Eversley asked where his friend was. "For it's strange he didn't come in. You know he's growing moodier each day. Don't like the looks of things." He shook his head.

"Oh, I wouldn't put too much value on it," Charles answered, "though he does seem to be under a certain constraint. Still we all have our moments, and I wouldn't place too much importance on it. I am the guilty one, though, for he charged me to make his regrets to the ladies and I forgot."

"But he does plan to come with us tomorrow?" Melinda asked.

"Oh yes, no problem to that, although I am not sure he is clear that it is his coach that has been offered. Now, what else is there to see but the Norman church?" He turned to Elizabeth. "Don't take it amiss, my dear, but I've seen that church at least once a year for the last four and forty."

"Charles," Elizabeth replied, laughing, "then I would say your duty is done. You may sit by the fire in the village inn while we investigate it thoroughly."

Elizabeth enjoyed antiquities, much to the discomfort of most of her friends. Melinda warned Lord Eversley that she was going to join Charles, but he was confident he would be able to keep Elizabeth's visit down to a short one.

They talked about the village and the Neivens, and then Evers announced that a small luncheon was ready. His lordship's proper half-hour call was to the winds. He was pressed to join them and he did.

After a merry time at the table Melinda announced she was going to treat Lord Eversley as if he were an old friend, to which he replied that she must call him "Richard" and Melinda in turn asked him to address her as "Lindy," and dear Elizabeth would prefer to be called "Beth." Elizabeth smiled politely. Melinda said that both she and Beth were truly exhausted and needed a rest and that the gentlemen must excuse them.

Eversley began to take his leave, but as both he and Melinda were easily drawn off onto tangents, it was only after Charles rose and wished Eversley a good ride that he went.

Elizabeth did not linger with her friends to talk over Lord Eversley. Pleading genuine fatigue, she went upstairs to her room. She vowed she would be strong; she would not cry. Her heart did not hurt because he did not want to see her; she was not in pain. Yet tears might have relieved her, for her dreams were of despair, darkness, and loss.

It was time to dress for dinner when Elizabeth opened her eyes. Fretty already had laid out the brown wool dress for her. Elizabeth barely had a chance to wonder what had happened to her resolution to leave this day, for Fretty kept talking, or reminding her that Lady Melinda was ready, or making her sit bone still as her hair was pinned.

After dinner, as they were talking in the green room, Elizabeth remarked that she would be out of clothes shortly. She had not thought she would be on display. "Are all country visits thusly?"

"Oh, I'm so glad you agree with me, Beth, for I think you need more clothes too. We'll have Fretty send for my little seamstress who can whip up some pretty day frocks. I should have thought of that before. But we should have the evening ones done at the dressmaker. There is a limit to how many shawls you can put around a gown to make it look different."

"To your little seamstress, yes, thank you, Lindy, but I will not have more evening frocks. You forget my life is not going to be a round of parties."

"Oh nonsense, Beth! No one can be more useful than Mrs. Hubert Creighdon, and you notice that she is always up to snuff. Who said you had to do good works and look as if you came off the Poor Rolls? Why, even our parson's wife is better dressed than you were in that horrible thing you wore when you arrived! I meant to ask you, when your clothes came from Margate, what did you do with them?"

"It is true, they were not very happy clothes, were they? I asked Fretty to take most of them and give them to the poor."

"Well, they won't thank you!"

"Lindy, you are terrible!" Elizabeth was laughing as was Charles who had been listening to the exchange.

"Well, I choose to think that I am sensible," was Melinda's answer when she could speak. "Now, you look so tired, dear, you must be off, for tomorrow we want to shine. Two gentlemen in attendance; no, I will have no faces made. It is a flattering thing! Oh, I know you have no interest in either, but show me a woman who in her heart is not pleased by attention from a gentleman, and I'll show you a dead one!"

Elizabeth was interested in the morrow; she would see Edward and that had become very important to her. She could even see some humor in the situation, for Lindy thought she was interested in Lord Eversley and indifferent to the duke. *Au contraire,* it was as she had known from the beginning; it was he who felt nothing for her. Elizabeth would not enlighten her friend.

Chapter Twenty-two

The next morning there was a thin layer of snow on the ground. It did not appear that more would fall, but there was a sharp wind off the Channel, and even Charles, who was used to the rigors of the Peninsula, admitted he would be glad to ride in the coach.

Both Melinda and Elizabeth dressed warmly, Melinda in a stomacher front gown of dark green wool and Elizabeth in a deep blue wool frock with a light green silk chemisette. Melinda made Elizabeth borrow her dark blue wool cape and insisted that they wear bonnets, not hats, for she had been exposed to the icy interior of the church before. Charles looked dashing in his greatcoat, or like a highwayman, depending on whether one listened to Lindy or Beth.

The coach arrived at exactly ten. Both the duke and Eversley were in trousers, which Melinda privately told Charles probably was the London fashion rather than his breeches, but reminded him she loved him whatever he wore. Danforth seated the party. Melinda went in first, followed by her husband, and then Elizabeth. Eversley was waved in and found himself in front of the Hanthornes. Danforth entered and ordered the carriage off.

Elizabeth knew that some time she would have to look at his grace, but it was awhile before she could raise her eyes to his handsomely tied cravat. Eversley thought she looked very fetching; Danforth felt the same and was determined to put her at ease. He would be as conciliatory as possible; his goal was to repair their friendship. After general comments on

129

the weather he began to relate one of the many stories concerning his Aunt Sarah.

She was a great one for improving her properties
and had embarked on a rebuilding scheme which
would make the whole estate "more natural," which
all of his listeners understood to be quite the fashion. In pursuing this, she determined that a small
hill behind her stables had to be raised, and while
this was being done, it was discovered that all of
the earth had been covering a Roman manor house.
She'd instructed the workmen to remove each shovel-
ful of earth as carefully as if they were bridegrooms
removing the garments from their maiden brides—
but in language more lusty, for she belonged to the
previous generation which believed in speaking
frankly.

She conferred with the Vicar, an antiquarian who
was sensible enough to agree to all of her proposals.
Together they planned to move the building to a
site in her gardens overlooking the river. And she
did not really like the way the manor had been laid
out, so she rebuilt it to be more in keeping with what
a Roman manor on her property should be. She had
added a few rooms, had marble brought in for simple columns.

When it had been assembled to her liking, she
invited her friends and those of the country worthy
of the honor to a grand party. She decreed that all
come in Roman attire; their menu was what she
felt a Roman patrician would serve her guests; and
the dancing was held in the ruin. It was proclaimed
one of the most comfortable Roman houses they had
ever seen.

Everyone laughed, even Elizabeth who had been
horrified at the cavalier treatment of a relic. While
she spoke her indignation, she found that she was

looking straight into Danforth's eyes, and her voice faltered. Melinda, who did not agree with her, started to tell her so, and the awkward moment was covered. The house was not being used before; his Aunt's rebuilding of it in a better location and in a nicer manner was quite reasonable.

While Melinda spoke, the duke was able to softly speak to Elizabeth. "It was not so difficult, was it?" he asked, smiling. Elizabeth tried to keep from blushing, but she could feel her color rising.

To bring the others' attention to himself, he began to recite:

> "The Rainbow comes and goes, and lovely is the Rose,
> The moon doth with delight, look round her when the heavens are bare,
> Waters on a starry night, are beautiful and fair;
> The sunshine is a glorious birth; but yet I know, where e'er I go,
> That there hath pass'd away a glory from the earth."

Elizabeth recognized the lines and, as he had hoped, forgot her own embarrassment. "That is almost what I mean, but more precise is: 'Men are we, and must grieve when even the shade, of that which once was great is pass'd away.' "

"Oh, that's not fair!" Melinda protested. "At least you, Beth, and you, Charles, know that I am not bookish! Not that I am trying to make them blue stockings, for I'm not, but it isn't right that you should argue with me from Shakespeare!"

Charles, Danforth, and Elizabeth laughed. "My love," Charles explained, "they were quoting Wordsworth, not the bard. I leap to your defense. 'All, all of piece throughout; Thy chase had a beast in view; Thy wars brought nothing about; Thy lovers were all untrue. 'Tis well an old age is out, and time to begin anew.' "

Elizabeth felt it was time to change the subject. "But, dear Lindy, you do know music, while both Charles and I have tin ears."

Lord Eversley had been letting most of the recitation of poetry go by, but he could tell by Melinda's expression that she was not happy. He caught Elizabeth's last few words and took Melinda's hand saying, "We all have tin ears, my lady."

Charles and Melinda both tried to set him straight, as the duke and Elizabeth sat quietly, feeling very kindly toward each other. At last the duke said, " 'So love was crown'd but music won the cause,' which Lady Hanthorne, was Dryden's answer to us all."

Really, Elizabeth thought, this is what I wanted; for us to be on these terms, as friends, and she looked up to find the duke's eyes on hers. Neither could do more than look intently at the other.

Melinda was talking, and it wasn't until she called Danforth's name that their time was broken.

"—for I do know one. 'Think of this, and rise with day, Gentle lords and ladies gay!' Which is what we should be doing!" And she beamed at them all.

Harmony restored, they arrived at the Neivenses'. Lydia met them, saying that only she would take them to the church, for her husband, as justice of the peace, was busy settling the case of a poacher. "He will join us for lunch, for even Mr. Godwin will have to stop talking sometime."

Once again they reentered the carriage for the short drive to the village. They drew up in front of the vicarage and a short, bent older man came out to meet them. Lydia introduced them to the Vicar, Mr. Bennington, who was delighted to have interest shown in his love, the old church.

Charles remembered a quiet, sheltered seat in the cemetery adjoining and made for it, while the rest of the party walked to the western entrance of the church, where Mr. Bennington gathered them closely around him and began:

"Now, first you must understand that this present church only dates back to the twelfth century and replaces the Saxon church which was built here, as much as we can determine, on or around 935. William gave this manor and another one nearby to one of his companions, a Robert of Arles. Unfortunately he was killed by a kinsman of the wife of Robert of Gloucester before he could do more than raise the Saxon church. There has been speculation and much correspondence among the members of the Royal Society, that it was for this reason he was killed, and not because he was a supporter of William Rufus; but"—and he paused for a moment sadly—"I am afraid that we really shall never know."

Lord Eversley tried to catch the duke's eyes but could not.

"Howsoever," the Vicar continued, "his son, William, was more interested in his holdings in the north and apparently did nothing about the matter of the church here, but *his* son, Henry, who also was a supporter of Beauclerc, was conscious of his obligations, and so had work commence in 1120."

Lord Eversley discovered Charles's absence. There was a great warring in his soul between his desire to escort Elizabeth and his common sense, which called Mr. Bennington a proser of the worst sort.

"—and so it was finally completed in the year 1132."

Before the party entered the fine western door, they were told to note the two severe towers flanking it and the large perpendicular window over the door. "Nave," "transepts," "circular clerestory windows," "Norman piers," and "lofty triforium" swirled around Eversley and Melinda. He could not see Mrs. Neivens now either. The duke and Elizabeth were impervious to the boredom of their friends. But Eversley held out—until at the font and the "stone carving, unfortunately, is late fifteenth century," and he was broken.

"I say, Lady-er-Lindy," he whispered, "enough's enough. Although," he hastily added, "I can see that it is all very interesting."

"Yes, yes, I agree, but let us see where Charles has been able to hide. We can slip out through the north door," Melinda whispered back.

One last chance. "But the others?" he asked.

"Look at Beth!" Melinda hissed back. "Do you think you could drag her away? No, never, for she is enjoying it and would not thank you, so do let us go whilst we can." She took him by the hand and began to lead him out the door. He looked back once, but the others were engrossed in the story of a fire set during the time of the Protectorate and how a certain John Buxton braved the mob. They ever so quietly opened the door and slipped out.

The duke was aware of his friend's discomfort and had been counting on it, for he knew Eversley's tolerances as well as he knew his own. Danforth was resolved to be on easy terms with Elizabeth again; it would be much easier without Eversley's presence.

It was almost another hour inside the church, and then they followed Mr. Bennington out the south porch to look at the early gravestones.

"We, um, speak of ninth through the thirteenth as early. And in this I think we are within our right, for there is independent verification, for the records were well preserved. That is not the case with Inchby which claims much earlier ones; but as I have repeatedly told the Rector, merely wishing does not mean proof. Proof, man, proof!" and he clenched his fist, daring anyone to take up the spurious claims of Inchby.

Elizabeth spoke soothing words, the red receded from the Vicar's face, and he became apologetic. The duke asked about the newer graves, and Mr. Bennington led them over, explaining the problems, especially those encountered in the 1666 plague that devastated the village. They also met the others of their party, who were quite chilled by now. Mr. Bennington was concerned, but Elizabeth reassured him that it had been a very interesting tour. They were invited to the vicarage for tea and to examine several old records, but Lydia made excuses as Mr. Neivens was waiting at the manor, and with the utmost professions of gratitude, they departed.

Lord Eversley held his indignation until they were on their way, when he turned to the duke. "Want to speak to you, Edward," he said.

The duke was at peace with the world and could sympathize with his friend, to some extent. "Of course, Richard, of course," he answered, but then could not resist teasing, "What an excellent idea it was. This was one of the most interesting Norman churches I've toured."

Eversley could only sputter. Charles laughed, saying, "Not his fault, Eversley. I think that I did warn you about Elizabeth."

"Why, Charles, I protest," Elizabeth said. "The

Vicar was fascinating. Did you know that the pews, though of the sixteenth century, were carved by men from this village?"

"Yes, my dear, I'd heard tell of it. I'm sorry you missed that point, Eversley, but I really thought you and Lindy would give them the slip sooner. Lydia wandered out after giving the nave a once-over."

"Certainly we could have done so," Melinda said, "and run the risk of getting a worse chill than we have now! There is a certain coldness to be found in the stone benches in churchyards that is not to my liking. Lydia, I hope you have a roaring fire, for I'm chilled to my bones!"

Lydia reassured them the fires would be large, and they arrived at the Neivenses' again. The ladies were led away by Lydia to freshen up and the gentlemen followed George to a small sitting room where there was a large fire and a large silver punch bowl. Their host immediately called for the hot rum and by the time the ladies rejoined them, the smell of cloves, cinnamon, lemon, and rum filled the room.

They all stood around the fire with steaming cups in their hands.

"This for me is the best part of the expedition; good friends, good fire, good drink," and Melinda raised her cup to the rest.

"Good Lord, Lindy," Charles remarked. "You sound just like one of my subalterns!"

"And where do you think I heard it?" his wife responded saucily.

"Here, here, Lindy!" Elizabeth echoed. "Who is to say that ladies can not appreciate 'the finer things' too?" And she raised her cup.

"Well said, Mrs. Campbell," Danforth said, raising his. "But I am not sure that we all might agree on what are the 'finer things.'"

"Sir, you knew very well that I meant it is possible for us to enjoy a morning spent in the company of a fine antiquarian and equally enjoy the companionship here in this room."

"Ah, as long as you state 'equally,' my dear lady. We should all strive for the golden mean," Danforth said piously.

"If you will remember, sir, Mr. Bennington was a man of passion in his beliefs." The duke smiled and she repeated, "In his beliefs. Not a 'meek shall inherit the earth' man at all!"

"My dears," Melinda protested, "we don't know what you mean."

"Dear lady, you too must hear of the Inchby claims," the duke said.

"Oh, no," laughed Lydia. "Do you know that Mr. Bennington almost came to fisticuffs with their Mr. Withers? George, please do relate the story."

George agreed, but as the tale was a long, involved one which made George stand on his chair at one point, lunch was announced before it was done, but as the punch bowl was empty, all were ready to move into the dining room, where George agreed to continue it.

Chapter Twenty-three

An exceptionally good claret was served, as was the conclusion of the Inchby claims, and by the time the sweets were passed, all were on a first-name basis. Lord Eversley was impressed. He turned slightly glazed eyes to his host and asked, "George, how can you remember all of that?"

Lydia answered, " 'Tis no puzzle at all. What he does not remember, he makes up." Everyone joined in the laughter, even George who admitted there was a bit of truth in his wife's statement.

"But you must know," said George, "that as justice of the peace, many of these items come before me. And through Crownenshield of the Royal Society, I am kept informed to their position."

Danforth and Elizabeth started to speak at once, and the duke nodded to Elizabeth to continue. "Lord Crownenshield was a close friend of my father."

"Crownenshield and my father carried on a correspondence for years," Danforth said in turn. They stared at each other.

"I don't see why that should be so odd," Charles commented. "What would be unusual would be if you had no one in common. People of our class are either related to each other, or our mothers came out together, or our fathers took the tour together."

Lord Eversley, unappreciative of the growing rapport between Elizabeth and the duke, asked, "Ain't you overdue in town, Edward?"

The duke looked at him. "No," he drawled, "not in the least. Though I had thought you were going up for the Henshaws' Ball?"

They eyed each other as two blood stallions scenting the same mare. The table was quiet, then Melinda spoke. "We made our excuses to the Henshaws, but we positively must be up for Lady Meddlemark's fete." She included the whole company, "Charles is right about everyone knowing everyone, for Lady Meddlemark was my mother's bosom friend. We are trying to talk Beth into accompanying us."

Her last sentence was of interest to the two men and they turned to Elizabeth, who shook her head. "No, I do not intend to go. That is not my world, nor do I wish it to be. I love you, Lindy, but I would not be happy there."

"A home for distressed cabin boys, open only to those between the ages of eight and ten with fathers who were former chimney sweeps, would be more to your liking?" the duke asked gently.

Elizabeth promptly took up the bait. "And I suppose your thoughts for my life would be more appropriate? You are remarkably good at knowing what others should do—if it agrees with your wishes!"

They glared at each other as if they were back alone in the bedchamber, their two weeks apart like a mere two hours, their underlying passion rising to the surface again, the others forgotten.

"Capital, Edward," Elizabeth said demurely, the better to provoke him. "Now that I know my future is in such capable hands, I may be at ease. I assume that each of your companions receives her own establishment? I would prefer mine with a garden, for I do enjoy working with the flowers."

He reacted to her outrageous goading as she had intended. His face livid with rage, he rose to his feet; she too half rose to meet him. Charles was the only one able to break out of his shock, and he put his hand on Elizabeth's arm. She was surprised at the touch and turned. The sight of his face broke the spell, and, shaking off his hand, she rushed out of the room.

Danforth prepared to follow, but Charles cleared his throat and the duke paused, regarding him thoughtfully. Melinda slipped out of her seat and went after Elizabeth. Danforth turned to his host. "My complete apologies, sir. If I might have the loan of a horse? It is time that I left. My sincere apologies, ma'am." He bowed to Lydia, nodded to the other men, and followed George out of the room.

Charles sank back into his seat. Lord Eversley shook his head. "Don't know what to say, Charles, Lydia, don't know what to say. Why, he and Elizabeth don't even know each other; it was her husband he knew. Don't understand it at all!" He looked hopefully at Charles for enlightenment.

Charles managed a small grin. "No use looking at me as if I were a crystal ball, Richard. I don't know anything more than you. Brain fever? No, it seems that they both have a temper." He turned to Lydia. "My dear, this ill returns your kindness of today. I am very sorry."

Lydia murmured something and went to find the other ladies. They were in the upstairs sitting room. Melinda was attempting to talk to the white-faced Elizabeth, who just stared into the fireplace.

"—and whatever possessed you to even think of a subject like that, much less ever speak of it, and to his face too! Beth, what happened to you? Why? I don't understand!"

Elizabeth shook her head. "You cannot reproach me more than I can do myself. There is nothing you may say that I am not saying to myself. Oh, God in heaven, why?" Her voice rose, and she looked wildly at them both.

Melinda put her arms around her friend. "My love, I'm sorry to rip into you too. Come now, we will help you compose yourself."

"Lindy, you are all kindness and goodness. I am not. I am bitter, angry, and at this moment, filled with loathing—for me as well as for him. He did bait me, you know?"

Lydia judged it time to intervene. "I don't think it will do any good to agonize about it. You are among friends. Do try to help yourself, dear Beth. If we might help in any way, we shall. Would you like to lie down?"

"Lydia, you are Charity herself. I've ruined your lovely luncheon. I've—"

She was interrupted by the maid, who said their carriage was ready. Lydia went to Elizabeth and held her for a moment. Elizabeth accepted the embrace but could not return it. "Come, my dear," Melinda said as she took Elizabeth's arm. "We shall have you home in no time." At the door Elizabeth tried to apologize to George and Eversley, but she had difficulty speaking, and both told her not to try; they understood.

The ride back was immeasurably long. Melinda was bursting with questions for Charles, but he had given her such a look that she remained silent and sat holding Elizabeth's hand. They arrived, and Elizabeth looked at Lord Eversley. "My apologies, sir," she said in a very low voice.

Inside the house Elizabeth turned to her friends. "I know that I owe everyone an apology and an explanation. May we talk in the morning?"

Charles answered for them. "Up to bed with you, child. Fretty will tuck you in. It's been more than a full day." He bent and kissed her.

Melinda hugged her, and Elizabeth ran up to her

room. Melinda was going to speak, but Charles fore-stalled her. "Later, my love." He ordered Evers to bring them tea and Mrs. Frenshaw to be sent to Elizabeth and took his wife to the green room.

Fretty undressed Elizabeth, tucked her into bed, and gave her tea, but it was a long, long time before she could sleep.

In the green room Charles had kept his wife on other subjects until the door closed behind their butler for the last time, then she began and the ground she covered took her a good three quarters of an hour.

Elizabeth should now be a different woman from Ian's wife. But to be so inconsistent, so obstinate, so different, so strange?

Did Charles remember the New Year's Eve cele-bration? It was the ever-thoughtful Elizabeth who had made sure the Pipers were well taken care of. Did Charles recollect Lady Margaret's dilemma and that it was Elizabeth's tact which soothed? When Lawton's favorite hound was stolen . . .? She could go on, and did, with further examples of Elizabeth's superior qualities. Elizabeth had been an excellent hostess; she knew the duties of a guest; Beth was a considerate friend . . . why, even now, it was un-thinkable, the scene at the Neivenses'!

Why had Beth taken such aversion to the duke? They'd both enjoyed that horrible church. The ride to the Neivenses' had been unexceptional.

Would poor Eversley take fright? How affable, an easy temper, such good manners. What a contrast to his Grace! Richard was all understanding, a perfect match for her.

Could Beth have been bowled over by the atten-tions? That would not explain it, or would it?

While Melinda was talking, Charles was thinking. His conjectures might seem preposterous, but if he were correct, it explained Danforth's moods, yesterday's odd interview, and the angry man at the Neivenses'. It would more than account for Beth's humors too, and might give another understanding to their meeting in the hall. However, until either of them cared to discuss it, it would be far wiser not to mention it to his dearest wife.

"My, Charles, do tell me what to think because I make no sense of it at all!" Melinda sighed.

"I think, my love, that we can make no adequate judgment unless we know more of the facts than we now possess. Elizabeth is a dear and valued friend, and until she can—or wishes—to tell us what this is all about, we must wait and not be Paul Prys. As you say, it makes no sense. Come, let us turn our attention to more interesting things." And he took her up to their room.

Chapter Twenty-four

Elizabeth had two dreams which alternated during the night. In the first she was chased by fiercely arrogant hussars, mounted on large, coal-black stallions who pursued her across the countryside. It did not matter where she fled, they followed. Sometimes she went up through hills covered with spring flowers. She tried old oak woods, where wild boar scattered at her approach; once it was along the coast following the sand, until she reached a secluded bay—even through a deserted Sussex village with its neat gardens and trim fields—the ending always was the same. When she was exhausted and could run no more, a hussar would leap from the saddle, throw her to the ground, roughly pushing up her skirts, and brutally take her with his strong, hard body.

The other was in an elegant bagnio, where after being bathed, perfumed, and gowned in pure Italian lace, she sat—afraid that no man would want her, terrified that some man would. At last she was called and she was led to a room done in white and gold with long, full mirrors on one wall. There was a bed the size of a coach in the middle of the room and standing in front of it was Edward. He walked over to her and took her by the hand and slowly led her to the huge bed. He began to undress her, deliberately removing only one garment at a time, smiling at her and lazily exploring her body with his hands, gently caressing her with his lips, taking her with his eyes until she begged him to take her with his body.

They certainly were not the dreams of a proper

gentlewoman—Elizabeth was no child; she needed some good hard work. But the embarrassment stayed with her until memories of yesterday's scene superseded them. How could she have done it? She would have to make Danforth an apology—Edward being too intimate a name for this morning—and one to the Neivenses too. After yesterday's excessive emotion, the revealingly lewd nightmares, and this morning's mortification, Elizabeth was tired, but she would write her notes immediately.

The duke had been all pleasantness in the coach and during the tour of the church. It was as if there had never been a disagreement; the *amistad* which had grown during their enforced stay together continued to develop. He had shown regard for her; they had laughed together; they had enjoyed the same things. Even when they were in the Neivenses' sitting room, one of his toasts had been very amusing. She stopped.

She began to recall exactly what she had to drink. There had been two cups of hot punch—no, three. She had allowed her wine glass to be refilled at lunch. He had goaded her before, and she had answered him, but never had they been in the company of others. *Tonta!* Fool! Yes, he had blatantly provoked her, but she was a lady and knew how to behave. She had had too much to drink.

Words of her old nurse came into mind, verses she'd quoted when Elizabeth needed to be reproved: "And it shall be, when he shall be guilty in one of these things, that he shall confess that he hath sinned in that thing."

Elizabeth had insulted him to his face; she must apologize to his face. Edward was a very proud man, too much so at times, but she had overstepped the mark; it was she who was wrong and must admit it.

145

Elizabeth went to the wardrobe. It was a pity her new riding dress was not finished; she would have to wear Lindy's old one. It was not that she cared to dress that he might find her attractive, but it was more comforting to be dressed to the nines when in a difficult situation. She dressed. A last look in her mirror showed a pale woman dressed in a deep green habit. It was time to go.

Chapter Twenty-five

At Swatow Hall the duke was still sleeping. He had ridden home on his borrowed hack, furious with Elizabeth. He had used his skills to put her at ease; he had been charming, and for a while he had been very much in charity with her. To think that he had risen in the morning contemplating marriage with that infernal Xanthippe! His first impulse when he had seen her at Hanthorne's should have been obeyed —a slow, lingering torture at his hands was good to think on. He had wished to be gentle, had been ready to ask her forgiveness—fool!

By the time he arrived at his door, the edge was off his fury, and he appeared outwardly calm. He ordered a bottle of brandy for the library, changed it to two, told Dodson, his butler, that he would be leaving in the morning, said he did not give a damn what the cook did with dinner as long as no one tried to serve it to him, and stated he was not to be disturbed. Dodson had seen angry men before, the old Admiral having been a testy customer, but never had he seen a man consumed with such fire.

After serving the brandy and being peremptorily dismissed, Dodson had hurried up the back stairs to his wife's sitting room, where Parker was enjoying a bottle of port. Dodson and his wife, the housekeeper, had been trained by the Admiral and his lady, but now that Dodson was in the duke's employ, the old man had become accustomed to discuss with, and defer to, his grace's valet, who had been kind enough to advise him in many a situation.

Clearly this had been one such time; happily both

Mrs. Dodson and Parker were able to perceive this as he entered the room. Both glasses were put down, and Mrs. Dodson roused herself from her chair and went to the cupboard, returning with a bottle of brandy and three glasses.

"Dodson, you must have something restorative," Mrs. Dodson said as she poured a hefty glassful for her husband and two slightly smaller ones for Mr. Parker and herself.

Dodson drank it, throwing back his head and letting the burning liquid rush down his throat. He looked up hopefully, but his wife was no longer looking at him but at Mr. Parker, who as befitting such an important occasion, cleared his throat and said, "There is something amiss, I perceive, Mr. Dodson."

"How kind of you to notice, Mr. Parker. Yes, as you so ably put it, 'something's amiss.' " He waited. Mrs. Dodson looked concerned, but impatient, so he judged it well to continue, "His Grace," he said and, having shared his solemn secret, he lowered his head.

Mrs. Dodson felt the announcement called for more brandy. After it was poured, Parker again cleared his throat, but Dodson could not wait.

"It's this way, Mr. Parker. His Grace came in, alone, half an hour ago, looking like thunder and lightning. He ordered a bottle of his best for the library and then made it two. Told me you would be leaving first thing in the morning, wants no dinner, and off he went to the library like he was the hanging judge and happy of it too!" He had paused to take a sip. "So, perceiving that all was not well with his Grace, I thought it wise to consult with you, Mr. Parker, for if you are truly going off in the morning, there is much to be done tonight with the maids to be told and the footmen to carry things, and Hoare must know . . ."

Parker was no longer thinking of Dodson's problems; he was considering those of his master. He had participated in the search in Margate and dealt with the duke's moods when it was unsuccessful. He had watched his Grace throw himself into the organization of the estate here in Kent and had been glad for Lord Eversley's visit. He had been prepared to leave several days ago when he received the countermanding orders.

There had been a change in the duke after the dinner at Greenfields. Parker had a talk with Hoare, who spent the long evening with the other coachmen and various Hanthorne servants to discover that Lord Hanthorne had a houseguest, a widow by the name of Campbell. Parker had thought it interesting that the duke had not mentioned that fact; that their relationship was no smoother than it had been in the north was also apparent. He had sent out a smiling, confident duke this morning . . . Parker resolved to take a greater interest in the matter. The present state of affairs was too unsettling for all.

Parker had been doubling as man to Lord Eversley—not that he would do the favor for anyone else, but he was quite used to his lordship and treated him in a fatherly way—thus he was aware of that interest in Mrs. Campbell. How that complicated things for his master, he did not know—as yet.

The Dodsons had been waiting while the valet sat thinking. Parker knew them to be decent persons, having worked in the family for years, but they should not be privy to his Grace's thoughts.

"Mr. Dodson," Parker said, "you were correct in bringing this matter to my attention. We can, howsoever, do nothing at this moment. Later I shall take it upon myself to ascertain what his Grace's wishes are."

Dodson was relieved, and both he and Mrs. Dodson thanked the valet. Mr. Parker consented to have some more brandy and was condescending enough to tell them several interesting stories of the great people that he and his Grace knew.

Down in the library the duke was like a raw youth, trying to become insensible. He was glad he had the foresight to call for two bottles. One was insufficient; one only heightened his sense of being wronged. One bottle brought Elizabeth clearly to him with remembered conversations complete to tilts of the head and gestures of her hands. That many of them had been arguments was true; she was an ill-tempered witch.

The second bottle had brought a different Elizabeth, the warm, kind Elizabeth, the Elizabeth whose wit was equal to any, the Elizabeth who was intelligent and sensible, the Elizabeth who was passionate, the Elizabeth he wanted.

What could he do? Either forget her entirely and go away, or forgive her again and win her—and make her beg his forgiveness. He rather liked the scene of her bending before him, tears spilling down her face onto her soft warm breasts, and he became confused. Was he sternly lecturing her on behavior or had he loosened her bodice so that her breasts were free, free for him to take in his hands and gently knead and then put his lips to them to kiss, to slowly cover them with his mouth . . . Damn it to damnation, he wanted her!

When Parker judged that the duke must be through at least half of the second bottle, he went downstairs. He opened the library door quietly, but his master did not notice his entrance. The duke was sitting in his favorite chair, his feet on the stool and his glass in his hand, staring into the fire. Parker cleared his throat before his master looked up. The duke had to clear the dreams of his lady from his mind before he could see the slight figure of his valet.

"And what the devil are you doing here?" he finally growled.

"You asked that I come at this time, sir," was the calm reply.

The duke looked at him for a minute or two. "The hell I did. I suppose you are going to say that I should be in bed?"

"No, sir, only that you would be more comfortable there. I shall carry the bottle if you require more."

"Damn it, man, you know I don't need more! No, you're right, I've had enough—although when I hired you to be a bear leader, I don't know. I am tired." He rose slowly.

The duke fell asleep easily into dreams that his soft pillows were Elizabeth's soft breasts. Parker noted the smile on his sleeping master's face before he blew out the candle and went out.

Parker returned to the Dodsons. "His Grace has retired for the night and does not wish to be awakened early," he reported. "At the present he has no definite plans for a departure, but his Grace, as befitting a man of his rank, has many commitments and may of necessity be forced to change his plans. If so, I will advise you." Declining another glass, Parker went to his own room, where he spent a short while thinking over the issue at hand, trying to make up his mind on how best to handle it.

Chapter Twenty-six

Elizabeth would speak with Melinda after she returned, for she had neither the time nor the inclination to think of what to say until her interview with Danforth was over. It was improper for an unescorted lady to call upon a gentleman no matter the hour, Elizabeth well knew—another excellent reason not to talk to Lindy until afterward.

She crept down the stairs as quietly as a mouse in a stable filled with sleeping cats and went to find Evers to give him her request for a horse, a good ride being what she needed. She would wait in the garden, for she wanted to see what yesterday's snow had done to the roses.

Elizabeth resisted the inclination to look back over her shoulder as she walked down the front steps, reminding herself that she was a grown woman, but she could not relax until she was into the garden and hidden by its hedges. She walked the paths near the entrance until the head groom led up the pretty chestnut mare Charles had assigned her.

He gave her a hand up and watched as she settled into the saddle and took up the reins. "I shall ride out by the old mill, Brown," she said. "I won't be needing you, so thank you." She smiled at him. "I don't know what time I'll be returning, but I shall take it easy."

Brown had seen her ride with his master and knew her to be a capable horsewoman, and as his mistress often rode unaccompanied on their land, he felt no unease in letting Mrs. Campbell ride alone. He saluted her as she rode off.

A morning call could not be made before eleven, another reason for Elizabeth to push on. With luck she could be there and back before anyone would see her. The mare was fresh, so Elizabeth let her out and enjoyed a run down the lane to the west of the buildings. Before the mare could tire, Elizabeth slowed her to a canter. They soon came to the site of the old mill and crossed the wooden bridge over the stream. Ice had formed in the eddies but the main part was still running. She would stop on the way back to enjoy it.

She followed a well-worn trail through one of the back meadows, picked her way through a coppice of mixed hardwoods, and some twenty minutes after leaving the house was at the boundary road between Greenfields and its neighbor. She could continue cross-country or take to the road, and she stopped to think.

The quickest way would be across, she decided, and trusting to her sense of direction, Elizabeth urged the mare on—over the hill, through an orchard, and across two more meadows. At a gate she dismounted and led her horse through, shutting the gate securely behind her before remounting. After she crossed the field, she could find no gate on the other side, and after studying the low wooden fence and the ground on the other side, she determined to give it a try. A pat to the mare and they were up and over. Her exhilaration could not last, for she had to watch the footing as they went through a marshy area. There was another meadow and then they entered another road, this time a well-traveled one.

From the description she had heard the duke give Charles yesterday, this should be the road in front of Swatow Hall. It would be more convenient if there were a signpost or an urchin saying, "This way to the duke of Danforth's estate," but though she looked in both directions, there was nothing except two crows high in a scraggly tree. She turned right.

An hour almost to the minute after leaving Greenfields, Elizabeth turned in between the large wrought-iron gates and started up the drive. She could have admired the trim hedges on either side had she not become suddenly preoccupied with what she was going to say to the duke.

An imposing Tudor house, with early Georgian additions greeted her. An alert stableboy ran up to hold her horse. She thanked him, dismounted, and walked up the steps to the front door. It was not the guillotine, nor was she an imprudent queen— just a foolish woman. She gave the knocker several hearty raps and waited.

Dodson opened the door; his eyes became wider when he saw she was alone. Elizabeth told him to take her name to the duke. As she clearly expected him to do so, Dodson bowed her in and asked to take her pelisse. She refused, saying that she did not plan to stay that long. Her knees were unsteady beneath her skirt; it was the ride, she told herself.

Dodson was in a quandary. She could not stay in the hall, but he didn't know where to put her. He was his master's surrogate in the reception of guests but this was a gentleman's residence and unattended females, though of obvious gentility, did not walk in the door demanding to see his Grace!

Parker shut the library door and came toward them. Dodson turned thankfully, his faith in the valet supreme.

Parker had immediately recognized Elizabeth. He came up to her and bowed. "Madam, permit me to say that it is good to see you."

Elizabeth was relieved to see him too. "Thank you,

Parker," she said, giving him a tight smile. "I wish to see the duke."

Parker nodded. "He will not keep you waiting long, ma'am." Turning to the butler, he advised, "Take Mrs. Campbell to the library, and I shall inform his Grace that she is waiting."

Thoroughly happy that the decision had been taken out of his hands, Dodson bowed to Elizabeth and led her to the book-lined room.

The large room had oak bookcases on three sides with long, small paned windows and a fireplace on the fourth. Some of the bookcases were original with the house; the others skillfully blended later additions. At the far end was a ball and claw-footed library table, while closer to the door were two red-velvet-backed Carolean chairs and a table. In front of the fire was a comfortable grouping of two barrel-shaped wing chairs, their footstools, and an upholstered sofa. If Elizabeth were on a tour, this would be one of the high Joints of the house. The oak paneling looked original too, for wood that mellow was next to impossible to duplicate.

Dodson entered with a tray. It was obvious from the reception Mr. Parker gave her that the lady was a valued friend. He still could not comprehend her unattended arrival. For a moment he wondered if she might be a follower of Mr. Robert Owens, for they were known to hold unconventional views, but he rejected that immediately; Mr. Parker would not have approved.

Elizabeth declined refreshment and Dodson left. She wanted to keep herself occupied whilst waiting so she started to tour the shelves and soon found herself truly diverted by the variety of the collection as well as some of the more improbable sermon titles. Each succeeding generation had added their own interests. There were sermons, religious tracts, questions of theology from the *Defense of Marriage of Priests* (1541) to a Methodist pamphlet of ten years ago. Memoirs, travel, volumes of Virgil and Homer in their original tongues, management of the estate, care of livestock and children; somewhere on the shelves there must be a book on any topic desired.

Parker had taken on the unenviable task of awakening his master; it was his duty. There would be an explosion, he had no doubt, for the duke's usual mood upon waking was unpleasant—excepting for those days when madam had been with them. He might wish that Mrs. Campbell had waited until the afternoon, but that was a thought unworthy of a man of his profession. Her visit was in all actuality just what his Grace required.

He opened the window curtains, which allowed the sunlight to stream into the room and onto the bed. Nothing. Next he opened the bed curtains. No response. He lightly touched his master on the shoulder. His Grace gave a little snore. He grasped the shoulder and shook it.

"Hellfire and damnation!" roared the duke as he sat up in bed. "What, if you love your miserable worm-infested life, are you doing?" He winced at what the sudden movement had done to his head.

"Sir, you have a visitor below."

"Damn all visitors! You woke *me* for that?" He glared at his valet, then gently lowered himself back on the bed to resume his sleep.

"Yes, sir, I took the liberty as I knew you would be desirous to receive her."

"Well I'm not! She could be the queen, and I would not care! Go away, Parker, go away *now!*" A strange look appeared as he remembered the pronoun. He looked up to his valet and demanded, "Did you say 'her'?"

"Yes, sir. Mrs. Campbell is below in the library and, while I am sure Dodson will take in a tray for her, I did not think that you would wish to keep her waiting." His eyes did not betray his interest in the duke's reaction.

"Hounds of hell!" The duke started to get out of bed, but his quick movement made his head throb again, and he sat for a moment on the edge. "Well, don't just stand there. Get me something for this head and put out my clothes, and get a move on!"

"I have a restorative here, sir. Please to remember that you do not care for the taste," Parker said as he put a tall glass containing a muddy grayish liquid into the duke's right hand.

"It's not the taste, Parker, it's the ungodly smell," the duke said as he brought it up to his mouth. He took a large swallow, choked, coughed, then finished it off in one long drink. "My God, you were right. The taste is worse," and he gave the glass back to his valet. His head, however, could be moved without extreme pain.

"Why did I drink so much last night?" he asked as he stood up. "It does not require an answer, Parker. Well, get moving, just don't jump around in front of me, man." He held up his arms to be helped off with his nightshirt. "And don't jabber at me either," he further warned. "My head isn't that good yet." He slowly proceeded to dress.

Parker suggested that if his master could continue without him for a moment, another glass might be advisable.

"Yes, yes, anything. Just don't natter," his master answered as he stood before the glass. Holding one of his beautifully ironed neckcloths, he started the very important task of tying it.

Parker returned by the time the duke was finishing the last fold on his fifth cloth, the other four lying on the floor where he had dropped them. He took the glass, downed it in one long swallow, wiped his mouth on the proffered cloth, then took a long look at himself in the glass. He turned to his valet. "Well, will I do?"

A black double-breasted coat, a gray and yellow striped silk waistcoat, and buff cord breeches—fit for a duchess, but Parker only said, "Yes, sir, very well."

Though his appearance was uppermost in his concern, the duke had thought about the forthcoming interview. If he could keep his blasted temper under control, and she hers, there might be another chance for them. *En avant*—forward!

He went down the stairs; Dodson was waiting in the hall. "Please see that I am not disturbed," he said as the butler moved to open the library door.

Elizabeth was at the far end of the room holding a slim red leather book. She looked up as he entered and waved it. "Oh, Edward! I am so glad you came! Was it an aunt or a cousin who left you this house? The library is positively amazing! Have you had time to look it over?"

His expression had been carefully neutral, but her enthusiasm made him break into a smile. He walked down the room to where she was still motioning to him.

"Why thank you, my dear Elizabeth. I too am glad that I came here this morning. Now, which other question should I answer?" He transferred the book from her hand to his left so that he might kiss her hand. He looked around, but there was no one else present.

"No, there is no one else," Elizabeth said, correctly understanding him. "Please do not say it, Edward. I know that I should not have come alone, but the thought of anyone else . . ." She reclaimed her hand. "Edward, sir, whatever you wish—it is difficult enough for me to do what I must do without worrying about some silly maid." She looked at him pleadingly.

"Do not look at me that way, my dear. We had a discussion once on that." He shook his head slightly. "Very well, but you have only five minutes, no more, before I call Mrs. Dodson. Woman, do you always fly all over the countryside alone?"

"You don't make it easy for me." Elizabeth's voice was low. "No, I do not want to sit," for he had gestured to the chairs in front of the fire. She moved a few paces away. "Please, do listen to me, and don't speak—and don't look that way at me either." Her face tightened as she fought back tears and refused to look at him.

"Elizabeth," he said and waited until she looked at him. He caught her hands and held them. "Elizabeth, do compose yourself, my sweet one. You came to see me, evidently for an important reason or you would not have come this early and alone. Come, my dear, speak frankly," and he held her eyes with his.

She tried to break her hands away, but he held them fast, so she took a deep breath and started. "I am here to apologize. It was all my fault." She could not help it, her eyes went down to his shoes.

His grip on her hands tightened. She heard his voice above her saying, "Elizabeth, it was my fault too. I was baiting you, you know."

She looked up. "Yes, I did know, and I could feel

my anger rise. But that does not excuse what I said. I am sorry."

The duke released her hands, walked to the window, and looked out. He took a deep breath, then turned back to her. "We both have damnable tempers."

"It's not only that, Edward," she said as she came over to stand in front of him. "I only realized it this morning. I had too much to drink too." She stood, meeting his eyes steadily.

He gave her a rueful smile. "Elizabeth, I think we should not refine too much on yesterday. I owe you mine for that last night, do you remember?" She continued to look at him, but she was pale. "Now, I listened to you; it is only fair that I be able to say to you—very simply, please forgive me, dear Elizabeth. I am very sorry."

"No more, Edward. I am none too calm." Elizabeth tried to smile.

It was with the greatest difficulty that he did not catch her in his arms. "Elizabeth, my dear, then I think we should make our amends to our hosts, a most charming couple, and let that be the end of it. What is far more important is this: I enjoyed the time with you. Can not we be on easy terms again?"

She could only smile her assent. He took her hand and kissed it gently before pulling the bell. "There will be other times to talk privately that will be better than now," he said, leading her to the fireplace.

"Then let me leave."

"No, my love, trust me in this."

Dodson entered. "Ask Mrs. Dodson to come to the library, please. Mrs. Campbell is especially interested in the ceiling. Mrs. Dodson can answer those questions better than I." Dodson promised that his wife would be with them promptly.

They were looking into the fire when Mrs. Dodson came in. She was happy to explain and show off the library, which was regarded as one of the show-places of its sort in Kent, or so Lady Langley had always told her. The plastered ceiling had leaves sprouting from mermaids, intertwined with sea horses, with grape vines interlacing the happy scene. The stuccoist was unknown but thought to be one of Charles Williams's disciples.

The duke spoke to Dodson again and returned to tour the room with them. He gave Elizabeth a glass of Madeira and raised his own to her in salute.

At last the duke turned to Elizabeth and said, "My groom is waiting to accompany you back, Mrs. Campbell. I still feel that you allowed Mrs. Hubert Creighdon to impose upon you, but I thank you for the message. It was important." He turned to his housekeeper. "My thanks to you too, Mrs. Dodson. You make an excellent guide." And he dismissed her.

Elizabeth thanked her too, for it had been interesting, even if she had not been particularly interested to learn all about his house that morning. She did not understand the reference to Mrs. Creighdon, but from his look she knew it was important to him.

Dodson was waiting to open the door. Before he let his butler open it, the duke spoke again. "My thanks again to Mrs. Creighdon, and more to you for having carried out her commission. No, no, there is no need to say a word more about it, Mrs. Campbell." He accompanied her down the steps to where a groom was waiting with her mare and another horse.

"Allow me," he said as she gave him her hand,

and he helped her into the saddle. He spoke softly so that they would not be overheard. "He has instructions to accompany you to at least the Hanthorne property. I would suggest cross-country, for both speed and circumspection. Say nothing about this, and I will pay a call this afternoon." His smile filled her heart for the entire ride back.

The duke straightened and became formal again. "A safe journey, Mrs. Campbell. I am in your debt." He waved her off, satisfied that he had quieted any interest in her unorthodox behavior—and that he would see her later.

He was entirely correct. At the mention of Mrs. Hubert Creighdon's name, all was instantly clear to the Dodsons. Mrs. Creighdon was as well known for her eccentricity as for her charity, and for involving as many persons into her plans as possible. That Mrs. Campbell was involved with her explained all; it made the visit an unremarkable one and not anything to be recounted later.

Chapter Twenty-seven

The return ride was uneventful. The groom left her at the boundary road, and while she was appreciative of the duke's solicitude, she was glad to be alone again. There were too many things which she wanted to think about. Elizabeth kept up a steady pace, for she knew that Melinda would be worried. She must also send off a note to the Neivenses this morning, but life was suddenly joyous again. She felt like singing and she did.

The mare was unaccustomed to the noise and shied, but Elizabeth had a good seat. It did not bother her; nothing troubled her—life was good! She remembered her promise to herself as she crossed the stream, but she could not linger now. Next time, mayhap with Edward . . . Then she was on the lane bringing her back to the buildings, and it was a very handsome woman who made the turn to the stables. Charles had just dismounted, and he watched her ride up.

He had gone into Ashford on business but, notwithstanding what he had said to Melinda yesterday, he was worried about Elizabeth. Without his pretty wife's distractions, he would be able to think. He knew Danforth's repuation, but try as Charles would, it looked like no flirtation that he had ever seen. Nor for that matter was it like any courtship either. Charles had more or less decided to put forward their trip to London and insist that Elizabeth go up with them. Then she came trotting around the corner to the stables. One look was enough to make him again realize the futility of planning around women. She was beautiful, not a line of care on her face. He'd take no odds that it was due to the ride she had just finished. Laughing at himself and his worries, he greeted her.

"Oh, Charles, what a glorious day!" she answered as he helped her down.

"Sure 'tis all of that, my pretty lady." He kissed her cheek. "And what a pleasant ride it must have been to put the fine color into your cheeks again."

Elizabeth blushed but told herself he could not notice. "Ah, I know when I am being quizzed, dear," she answered and took his arm for the walk back to the house. "I do owe both you and Lindy an apology for my execrable manners yesterday. No, don't interrupt," she said as he was about to speak. "You do know my behavior was inexcusable. I should not have had the punch and the wine both . . . Dear friend, please tell me how I can say that to the Neivenses?"

"Just the same way, my dear. Don't dwell on it. Send off your note. Make it as simple as you told me. They are an understanding couple."

"I know. I should hate to lose their regard, for, they are persons with whom I feel very comfortable."

At the front door Evers informed them that her ladyship had been worried about them both and was in the green room. Elizabeth excused herself to run up and change, saying rightfully that she was too horsey at the moment to even greet her mother. Charles, who knew his wife well, went off to the green room.

He was greeted by an uneasy Melinda. She was very happy to see him but, after she received his kiss, she began to tell him of Elizabeth's morning ride. It was with some difficulty that he was able to break into her words to inform her that Beth was upstairs and, far from being the distraught woman of yesterday, she was a glowing, radiant beauty. Melinda stared at him.

"Now, my sweet wife, if I might have your leave, I shall go upstairs and change. We shall be able to talk over lunch." He pinched her cheek gently and left.

After lunch and her apology to Melinda and further explanations of the need for her ride (to which Charles listened amusedly), Elizabeth went to her room to compose her note for the Neivenses. It was not as simple as it sounded. It is much easier to do so in person, she thought, but as Edward would be calling this afternoon, this would have to go by groom, and she made herself return to the composition. At last she was able to turn out something that she considered acceptable, if not exactly right, and before she could change her mind again, she went down to give it to Evers, who would see to its delivery.

Melinda had suggested that they take the carriage into Ashford or Canterbury and look for some material, but Elizabeth pleaded tiredness, and the expedition was postponed for the next day. She was indeed tired, but that had to wait as she looked over her gowns again, trying to decide what to wear for Edward's call. Fretty came in as she was holding the blue sarcenet up to her face to see how well it became her.

"I just knew you weren't resting as you should, Mrs. Beth! I just knew it." She took the dress and put it back into the wardrobe. "Now I want you to lie down and to stay there. Now, I'm not saying that it isn't good to have some exercise, but repose is necessary too." She put a pretty white coverlet over her charge.

"Now I know you are not a child, but there are times when you should listen to others that know, and this is one of them." She continued to softly scold as she went to the window and drew the curtains shut. Elizabeth knew Fretty was right, and she let herself sink into the bed and softly float into dreams.

When the duke was announced, Melinda was too surprised to say anything, and it was left to Charles to welcome him.

"And my compliments to Mrs. Campbell too. I owe all of you an apology for yesterday's rudeness and I have come to give it. Thank you, Charles," he said as Charles offered him a chair.

Melinda started to say that Elizabeth was resting and unfortunately could not be disturbed, but Charles interrupted her. "I don't think that she would mind being wakened."

Melinda rose to advise her friend, but Charles put his hand out and stopped her. "My dearest, let Fretty do it."

"But, Charles—"

"I know, love, let Fretty do it." Melinda sat down, and Charles went over to the bell rope and pulled it. "What would you like, Danforth?"

The duke had been amusedly watching the interplay between them and had correctly interpreted the unsaid parts. He laughed. "Anything at all, my dear Hanthorne—except a hot rum punch."

Charles laughed too, as did Melinda, somewhat belatedly.

Evers entered and Charles asked him to tell Mrs. Frenshaw that Mrs. Beth had a visitor. Then he might bring them refreshments. After Evers left, Charles and the duke talked of various and sundry things. Melinda tried to join in, but it was obvious her thoughts were elsewhere.

Fretty received the message and went to carry out the request. Like her mistress, she found it extremely interesting, but having had long experience with her master's judgment, she bowed to it as being superior to hers. As she looked at the sleeping woman, she tried to understand why the duke might be showing interest. As no ready answer came, she shook her head and gently awakened Elizabeth.

Elizabeth was refreshed and happy, but when told of her guest downstairs, she blushed, looked down, and then looked up at the watching Frenshaw. "Fretty, do help me; I want to look my best."

Fretty permitted herself a smile before she turned to the wardrobe. "Now then, Mrs. Beth," she said briskly, "why not the blue. You know it favors you."

Elizabeth got out of bed and began to first wash and then, with Fretty's help, put on the blue frock. Fretty kept up a steady stream of scolding which effectively kept Elizabeth's mind from the duke below and on the process of dressing above. Fretty insisted on doing her hair and, when the last strand was in place, looked her over and pronounced her ready to go down.

"And don't you keep putting your hand up to see that it isn't falling, because I've used enough pins to see that it isn't. Now, remember you aren't a simpering schoolroom miss. You are eight and twenty, not eighteen. Take this shawl," she said, giving a blue and red paisley to Elizabeth. "It will give you something to do with your hands." She sent Elizabeth off, but not before Elizabeth had turned and kissed her cheek.

Even with all of Fretty's words in her ears, Elizabeth was blushing again as she entered the green room. The duke bowed low over her hand and, still holding it, said, "Mrs. Campbell, my profoundest apologies to you. There is nothing that I can say, except please do forgive me, for I wish us to continue as friends."

Elizabeth's head and voice were low as she answered him. "Sir, you refine on it too much. I was equally at fault, and I beg your pardon." She blushed more as he pressed her hand before releasing it.

"Then I may call you Elizabeth again, and you will use Edward?" He waited for her reply.

"Of course, sir—Edward."

They continued to stand regarding each other, and Charles felt a bit of help would not be out of the way. "Come have a glass of Madeira, Beth," he said. They turned to find him smiling at them while Melinda watched them intently.

"Charles, I would prefer a cup of tea," Elizabeth answered with a smile as she walked over to the fire and sat down. Danforth also took a chair.

"Good heavens, Beth! What a hostess I am!" Melinda had been brought back to her duties. "Charles, please call Evers, and tea we shall have. What have I been thinking of?"

Evers came in, but before Melinda could ask for tea, he announced Lord Eversley, who followed him into the room. The duke and Elizabeth exchanged rueful smiles.

Charles greeted their guest and this time Melinda joined him in the welcome. The duke and Elizabeth began to speak to him.

"Ah, Richard, I owe you—"

"Lord Eversley, I do owe—"

Eversley, delighted to see that they had made up,

joined them. "Let it never be said that I was not prompt to do the same. 'Never a borrower nor a lender be.' " He looked at them expectantly.

"Sir?" Elizabeth began, "I fail to—"

Danforth, however, was used to Eversley's sense of humor. "Numbskull," he said rather fondly. "If you had let either of us finish, the last word would have been 'apology' not 'debt.' "

"Yes, but that ain't the way it came out. And it was clever," Eversley argued. Melinda laughed.

The duke turned to her. "Please do not encourage him, my lady. He gets beyond himself."

" 'Tain't fair, Edward!" Eversley objected. "You know if you'd said it, you wouldn't have had to explain it!" He looked to the others for support and they laughed again.

Elizabeth got up and walked over to him. "Dear kind sir, we truly are cruel, but I trust we have not hurt you deeply." He smiled at her and would have answered, but she continued. "We were, in all seriousness, trying to give you the apologies due you."

Lord Eversley took her hand. "My dear Elizabeth, chivalry is not dead. You are a member of that gentle sex which we are bound by law and custom to honor and protect. You would never need to apologize for anything."

Such a ridiculous statement, but Elizabeth could see he was willing to develop his theme *ad nauseam*. To illustrate the absurdity, she brought up her right foot and kicked him on the ankle. Eversley gave an involuntary yelp and looked at her in wonder, as did the others.

"Now, good sir," she asked, "you cannot tell me that I do not owe you an apology, and furthermore, that you would not promptly accept it?" Everyone laughed again.

Still laughing, Charles came up to them. "She has a point, Richard. Come, do sit and we shall protect you from further assaults from the 'gentler sex'!"

"Do you know," Melinda said thoughtfully as everyone sat down, "all of those knights rushing all over the country, taking maidens away from the wicked knights and then abandoning them. I've often wondered if those women wanted to be rescued by someone so dull. I do think I'd prefer an honest rogue to a pure, dull knight anytime!"

In the general laughter Edward's and Elizabeth's eyes caught and held for a brief moment. Only Charles saw it, for Eversley was earnestly explaining to Melinda what an improper course that would be.

"For my part," Elizabeth said, "I've often wondered where they found the models for such pure knights. The men that I have known, soldiers or not, were never that silly. Dedicated men, with completely human defects, but such fools, no."

"And I have met and known very resourceful women, for all of their outward appearances of fragility. I think of my Aunt Sarah, some of my farmer's wives, even a lady whose acquaintance I made in the North. All seemed to thrive in difficulties and wished no masculine help to extricate themselves."

Everyone had a comment to make, except Elizabeth. Tea arrived, with Evers and two footmen carrying large silver trays containing pastries, small meat pies, and confections. In the general confusion the duke found a moment to speak privately with Elizabeth.

"Ride with me tomorrow morning. I make a better companion than a groom."

"I protest, sir. He could not have been more correct."

"Ah but, my dear, I thought we had already determined that you too enjoyed the honest rogue."

At that, Elizabeth had to laugh, which made the other turn to her inquiringly.

"We were speaking of my Aunt Sarah again and her opinions of correct men and honest rogues," the duke explained glibly.

The two visitors soon took their leave, but not before Lord Eversley had a chance to speak to Elizabeth. "May I have the honor of riding with you tomorrow?" he asked.

"That would be a pleasure," she answered, "but Melinda and I are off to town tomorrow to shop."

He then went over to Melinda, who was with Charles and the duke, to discover where they were shopping, for he too had to be in town the following day, and perhaps they could have a luncheon together?

Melinda was going to accept when she caught Elizabeth's frown, and she smoothly changed to a vagueness as to their schedule and that all of their time must be devoted to their task. Eversley had to be content.

After the two gentlemen departed, Melinda turned to Elizabeth and demanded to know why she could not have accepted Lord Eversley's luncheon invitation.

Elizabeth had not cared to mention her ride with the duke but saw no way out. "Because, my dearest Lindy, I have accepted a ride with Danforth tomorrow morning."

"With the duke!" Melinda was startled. "Why, whatever for?"

"Because I wanted to, dear one. The only thing that troubles me is that my habit is not yet finished

171

by the seamstress, but at least the mare is first rate."

"That is a compliment, my dear," Charles thanked her.

"Oh no, it is not!" Melinda answered. She was willing to be diverted, for it was clear Elizabeth did not care to discuss the duke further. "The habit she is using is one of mine. Only the horse comes out well!"

"There is just one thing that should be mentioned," Charles said seriously. "You do know Danforth's reputation—and that it is a well-founded one. He is known for his flirts and for his women on the side. To my knowledge, he has never offered for anyone. I cannot imagine him offering you *carte blanche* but . . . Do you have any feeling as to his intentions? I do not mean to sound as if I am the ponderous older brother, but it must be considered."

Elizabeth looked steadily at Charles. "No, dear Charles, I do not know." She lowered her eyes. "I wish I could know, but I don't."

"Good Lord, Beth!" Melinda said, rising. "Has it gone that far?" She came to Elizabeth and put her hand on her friend's shoulder. "You barely know him!"

"I don't know anything, Lindy," Elizabeth answered. "All I do know is that I want to be with him. Oh—let us let it be. It will do no good to talk about it; there is nothing to do. I am sorry that you both are anxious about me, for I do not mean to cause you worry." She pressed Melinda's hand.

Charles rose and came to them. "Of course we have concern, for we love you too, Beth. But enough of that, or I shall sound like one of those rattly knights both of you so deplored." He took a hand from each. "Time to dress for dinner, I judge, although how any of us can be hungry, I do not know. Still for the wages I pay for the cook, we must all eat until we are more than stuffed." He brought them to their feet and gave each a kiss on the cheek. There were no further references to the Duke of Danforth that evening.

Chapter Twenty-eight

Snow fell during the night and lightly covered the ground and trees, and when the sun came up, the whole world sparkled. An hour later it was all gone, leaving dirty ground and stark trees.

Elizabeth was fortunate to wake in time to see the glistening landscape. It was as if she were looking over an enchanted world. "If I believed in good omens, which of course I do not, but *if* I did, I should say that this is a perfect way to start a day," she announced. "And it certainly wouldn't hurt to have something especially powerful on my side. No, Morgan le Fay, I do not want your love potion now, for the good fairies are protecting me!"

She swirled around her room, only becoming sensible to her surroundings when her bare feet became cold. "Ah, but if I were a young girl in olden days waiting for my lover to come, he would not have been like Edward. Except Lancelot was pure before Guinevere, and so Edward must have been awkward in his wooing—at one time. I would not have him change in any way!" she declared fiercely to her glass. "He would not be himself, and I fell in love with him!" The image grimaced back at her, and she felt a trifle silly.

Her dressing was hurried because she wanted her breakfast. But when she went down to the breakfast room, only Charles was there.

"Lindy is still in bed trying to make up her mind if she is coming down with a cold or just feeling her age. I do swear that is precisely what she told me,"

Charles explained. "I did manage to persuade her that there was nothing so very important to do this day and that she should have breakfast sent up. So, my dear, you find me at loose ends this morning and very happy for your company. In truth, a good brisk ride with you and Edward this morning would not be displeasing." He smiled ingenuously at her and raised his teacup.

Knowing very well when she was being roasted, Elizabeth declined to answer him but went over to the sideboard to discover if there were anything especially interesting under the covers of the silver dishes.

"Did you notice the view this morning, or were you not up in time?" he asked.

"Yes, I saw your beautiful Kentish countryside this morning," she answered.

Charles watched her fill her plate. "Well, I am relieved after all, Beth, for you know that a woman with such a keen appetite cannot be in love. Dear me," he said as she came to the table with her loaded plate, "you seem to have missed the pickled eel. It is the second to the last in that rather ugly Elizabethan dish."

She could not ignore this. "Now, that is enough, Charles. I was always a practical woman and you can not tell me that starving myself would be of any use to anyone. Besides, you must have forgotten that I loathe eel." She sat down across from him and prepared to eat.

"I always thought it was jugged hare, but of no matter. You could always take baskets to the poor or to the unfortunate soldiers and fill them with pickled eels, thus supporting the local industry and allowing you to get it out of your household."

She had to grin. "I do see, dear Charles, what marriage has done for you. You sound more like your charming wife each day!"

"My dear Beth, was it not Lovelace who said that a well-rounded wench was what he wanted in his arms? Which, if you can finish that plate, you'll be on the way to being—bearing in mind that your Edward likes the flesh."

"Charles! It is 'a sweet disorder in the dress.' You are bawdy this morning. A ride would be just the thing—but not with me." She shook her fork at him. "Go ride with your charming lady wife, or better yet, do you go upstairs again and consult with her." Their bantering continued as they ate. Elizabeth was wholly in charity with the world.

Evers came to announce that his lordship's agent had requested the favor of an interview with Charles. Charles groaned but got up from the table. He paused as he was about to exit and turned back to Elizabeth. "Do take care, my love, do take care." He smiled and left.

Elizabeth was touched by his concern but would not let herself reflect upon his words. If she cared to be ready when Edward arrived, she must rush. Each hour with him was precious time and must not be wasted.

In her room she began the serious task of making herself as beautiful as possible. If there were time after dressing and before his arrival, she would look in on Melinda. Then she chided herself for neglecting her friend.

Fretty arrived to help and to do her hair. "For you know, you did look right yesterday afternoon, but that is not the mode you desire for a ride. Now do sit still, Mrs. Beth. A lady don't fidget—especially when her hair is being done."

"Now that isn't precisely the fashion of the moment," Fretty said as she was almost finished, "but with hair so long as yours you might as well take advantage of it and use some in braids. Then, with the hat set on it, there'll be few who can outshine you—especially in this corner of the world." With her small talk and practicality, she again helped Elizabeth regain her poise.

"There!" Fretty announced as she finished pinning the braids to her head. Parts were braided, others were wound, and all was put on top of her head. Fretty went to get the small black hat with the two pheasant feathers at the side.

"Now do show her ladyship how well you look and then off with you as the duke is waiting below."

Elizabeth had started out the door to go to Melinda, but at Fretty's final words, she stopped. "Why didn't you tell me?"

"I did not tell you, Mrs. Beth, as there was no use. You weren't ready and it would only have made you squirm more. Now don't look like that. It isn't the first time you've gone for a ride with a gentleman, and it won't be the last. Just see Lady Melinda first." Happy to have had the last word, Fretty opened the door for Elizabeth.

Elizabeth found Melinda sitting up in bed wearing a very becoming rose-colored shawl around her shoulders and surrounded by stacks of letters, with others strewn all over the bedclothes. Instead of looking the invalid, she looked very much the picture of health and Elizabeth told her so. While she was doing so, she forgot her preoccupation with today's ride as she looked intently at her friend.

"Something's up, my dear, and you can't fog me. You don't have a trace of the sniffles!"

"Well, I had to tell Charles something," Melinda

answered, grinning widely. "Oh, Beth, I am so excited. I think I am expecting!"

Elizabeth gave a cheer and embraced her. "Now, and why can't you tell Charles? You know what it would mean to him."

"That is exactly why I am afraid to mention it until I am very sure. We have wanted a baby for so long—five years—and yet nothing happened. He even told me that it did not matter to him, that I was his life and if God chose not to give us a child, we had so much else to be thankful for and that never once did he regret marrying me—which I for one cannot believe because I do remember two times when I am sure that we both felt that we did not suit. But on the whole I do agree with him, but I also know that in his heart, he wants a child of his own—just as much as I do. So now, when it is a bit too early to be absolutely sure, how can I get his hopes up?" She looked appealingly at Elizabeth. Then her mood changed and she giggled as she thought of something else.

"On the other hand, my dear, I do have certain interesting signs which *do* lead me to think that I *am* with child. Fretty thinks so too," she said, as if this were the most impressive evidence.

"Lindy, my dearest friend," said Elizabeth warmly, "I am so happy for you—for you both. But do tell Charles, and let him wait with you; do not keep him in suspense." She smiled happily at Melinda.

"I really don't know, Beth. Women who are in an interesting condition must be catered to."

Fretty entered. "I thought so," she said grimly. "Mrs. Beth, you came in here to show my lady how nicely turned out you are this morning, and then take your leave. Lady Melinda needs her rest!"

They looked guiltily at each other and at Fretty.

"My heavens, Lindy—Edward is down below. I

must fly. Tell me that I look ravishing, and elegant, and done up to the nines, and wish me luck," and she bent over to kiss her friend.

Lindy reached up and pressed her hand. "You know that I do wish you luck with all my heart. Though why you need it for just a ride, I am not sure. Oh, love, do be careful!" she begged.

Elizabeth kissed her again. "I shall be careful, dearest Lindy. Please do not worry." She patted Melinda's hand and then went to the door. "Do rest and do *tell* Charles!" she ordered as she left.

As she went down to the stairs, she continued to think of her friend's good news, and she was able to greet the duke with more composure than the day before. Charles had brought him into the green room to wait, and both men rose as she entered.

"An excellent morning for a ride, my dear Mrs. Campbell," the duke said, bowing low over her hand.

She returned his smile and greeting. "A magnificent morning, sir."

Charles wanted to be helpful and made a suggestion. "You know, if neither of you would mind waiting for half an hour, I could join you. Just have to clean up a few things and then we could have a brisk gallop. Just the thing for a morning like this."

Elizabeth would not meet Danforth's eyes, so he was the one to reply for them both. "My dear Charles, of course you would be more than welcome with us. Unfortunately my gelding is still too full of spirit to allow us to wait that long. I have one of your men walking him, but he needs to be off. Horses, you know, must be catered to as if they were a fine wine—or a woman."

Charles smiled, but that brought Elizabeth's mind back to Melinda. "Speaking of fine women, Charles, Lindy hopes that you will look in on her."

"Of course, my dear, as you suggest. Ah well, then you will both have to appreciate the morning all the more as you will do it for me too." His large smile warmed them both.

The two took their leave. Charles had ordered Elizabeth's mare to be brought up and when they went down the outside steps, she was waiting too. Danforth paused a moment before helping Elizabeth into the saddle and looked the horse over. "She is a pretty thing," he said as he ran his hands over her. "Gentle but with an alertness about her. Not a quiet lady's horse, but then that would not please you either, would it?"

He helped Elizabeth mount, took his own horse from the groom, mounted, and turned to Elizabeth for directions.

"There is a lovely ruin of a mill that makes a pretty starting-off place—if you would care to see it?"

"My dear Elizabeth, I am yours to command. Do lead the way."

And so they started to retrace Elizabeth's ride of yesterday. As she did before, as soon as they were cleared of the buildings, they let their horses out. It was an exhilarating gallop for them both. When they slackened off, Elizabeth turned a radiant face to him. "Oh, Edward! That was splendid!"

He felt his heart catch again. The look in her face as she gazed up at him made him want to pull her out of the saddle and bring her to him. Telling himself to steady, he let out his breath, but his eyes showed the warmth of his feelings as their eyes remained fastened on each other. Elizabeth, who had forgotten she was on horseback, was brought back to the present when her mare abruptly stopped. Danforth quickly brought his horse back to her and asked if she was all right.

"Why, yes, although why she decided to stop . . ." And Elizabeth shrugged her shoulders rather than look up into his eyes again.

"That, my dear lady, is a prerogative of your sex. A man is taught from early childhood never to question the sudden changes in directions or the stops or starts of the distaff side."

"What nonsense, Edward. You for one are always questioning me as to why I do some of the things I do."

"Well, yes, but it is because I am interested in the reasons behind the actions. There is a difference."

"Sir, I am determined to be in perfect accord with you this morning—so do not try my patience. Fatuousness ill becomes you!"

"And that, my sweet, is what I do love about you. One is never sure in what direction either you or the conversation will take." He smiled, taking any sting from his words.

She tried to ignore his usage of the word 'love,' but her color heightened.

To change the subject, she abruptly asked, "Edward, do tell me, what do you know about hop growing?"

He stopped his horse and stared at her. "Hop growing? How in all that is holy should I know anything about hop growing?"

"My dear Edward," she answered, laughing at his blank look, "you are a university man. Surely one who is well educated should be able to enlighten me on a subject that is of the gravest importance to this county."

"Your trouble, my dear Elizabeth, is that your father neglected to beat you with regularity!"

"My father, sir," she retorted indignantly, "never once beat me!"

"And when you especially needed it?" he inquired kindly.

"Never! I would receive a short lecture on the obligations that I, as an intelligent being, had to the rest of the world, not the rest of the world to me. No, from the earliest my father used reason in place of the rod—not that there were not times when I would have preferred him to have beaten me, rather than seek to make me responsible for my deeds. For a beating would have been over and done with, but once I had to think—why, my mind would churn on and on.

"Our housekeeper would come for me and say either 'whatsoever a man soweth, that shall he also reap' or else 'what measure ye mete, it shall be measured unto you,' and then briskly tell me to finish my lessons, or whatever it was that I was supposed to be doing."

"Elizabeth, I find your father's approach most interesting," said Edward. "After an appropriate physical punishment my father would set me to think of my actions, and I did; as most of the things for which I was punished I heartily enjoyed doing, he canceled out the harshness of his sentence by the reflection."

"And what were you doing that you enjoyed it so?" she asked.

"I did the things that all healthy children should be doing—playing with other children, riding my horse, getting dirty. But, you see, when you are the son of a man who feels that dukes are not as ordinary men, these are not viewed as healthy or proper or befitting one's station in life. My lectures were not on the duties that intelligent beings owe to the world, but rather what my rank was due, and what obligations I had in order to continue the just order. My father would never have allowed your father in one of his livings. Seditious nonsense, he would have called it."

"And my father would have called your father one of those regrettable nobles who truly had forgotten the original purpose of his family and the aristocracy: to serve crown and country."

They had stopped some minutes ago, the better to continue the conversation. They sat considering each other and then began to laugh. He reached out to take her hand.

"How far afield we've gone this morning—in our talk, not our ride," he said. "Come, Elizabeth, show me your mill and I promise that I shall keep my late, unlamentable father under check if you will hold your estimable father under tight rein. I could not wish for you that we would have traded fathers, but I would have enjoyed knowing yours. A man of wisdom—even if he did produce a hoyden."

They set off at a walk so they could continue to talk. Although he refused to enlighten her on hop growing, he did talk of his family and of his loneliness in growing up and of the love that he developed for the land, which was encouraged by his father's estate manager.

"For the feeling that I have is as strong within me as that of a Saxon ceorl. In a way it is an inherent English love of one's native land."

"But, Edward, you spend so much time in London. Surely that time is not spent in walking through Kew Gardens?"

"Elizabeth, have I told you recently that you are a saucy wench! Is there no one that you hold in awe?"

She thought this over. "Yes," she answered thoughtfully, "yes, there are two: Lord Wellington and your Mrs. Hubert Creighdon."

He laughed. "Do you realize, my dear, that I have laughed more with you than with any other woman that I have known? No, do not stop me, but rather stay your horse a moment." She did. "We found that to be true in the few days we spent together in the North. Yes, I know I have enjoyed the company of other women, but in different ways and never have I found one with whom I am so compatible—and yet one who can infuriate me as you do. I was not going to say this now, but it seems to want to be said. We do suit each other well; Elizabeth, would you do me the honor of becoming my wife?"

His voice had become increasingly harsh until the last sentences were delivered in the stern voice that she had never heard before. Elizabeth felt a great pain in her chest, as if she were starting to break apart. This was what she had wanted, his proposal, but now that it was made, it was for the wrong reasons—because they suited, not because he loved her.

She could finally speak, but she could not control the tremor in her voice. "Edward, oh please, Edward —you should not have said it! Why could we not just be friends—and enjoy each other with nothing more than that? Husband and wife, never; friends, I had hoped for."

"That, my love," he answered with a harsh laugh, "is usually what I say to some woman who is importuning me." He looked at his horse's ears, but if she could have seen his eyes, she would have known the pain there. "Never mind, please don't let my untimely declaration come between us; we shall be friends and it is probably for the best that you refused me. Come, on with the ride. I have yet to see this mill which by now is almost a legend between us."

He turned to her, but this time it was she who regarded her horse. "Do not fret, Elizabeth," he said. "I will not cause you any more discomfort by alluding to it again. If it will make you happier, I will even discuss hop growing with you. I shall be all amiability." He laughed again.

Elizabeth nodded her head, and they started the horses again, this time at a trot. She looked at the barren winter scene, the jagged rocks without their mossy covering, the stark trees, the muddy fields, the indifferent sky. Try as she would, the word "compatible" kept ringing in her ears until she put her hand to her right ear to stop it.

The duke immediately noticed her move but, interpreting it as a sign that she was becoming cold, he suggested that it might be better to return to the house and continue their ride another day. She in turn, feeling that his suggestion was made to get rid of her, gave him a small "yes" and so they turned their horses back toward the house.

The ride was accomplished in silence, both obsessed with their own thoughts. Their horses sensed their riders' disquiet and were skittish.

Elizabeth's desolation was complete. She was riding beside him, but it was as if she were alone. She wanted him with all her being, and he had asked her to be his wife because they were "compatible." Her eyes filled with tears as she thought of the years ahead of her; without him there was nothing.

They arrived at the house; it was no more than twenty minutes, but it seemed as if half a day to the unhappy couple. She very formally invited him in, and he, equally formal, declined, citing business reasons at home. He helped her from the saddle; she thanked him for the fine ride. He thanked her for her company and took his leave.

Elizabeth gave her mare to a groom and entered the house.

Chapter Twenty-nine

Elizabeth wanted the sanctuary of her room, but as she came to the stairs, Charles was at the top. "Beth! Beth!" he shouted. "Don't come up—we must celebrate!" He took the stairs two at a time. "Lindy must rest, but we shall have a bit of the bubbly!" He gave her a bearish hug and drew her off to the green room. He pulled the bell for Evers, then paced excitedly, telling her of his jubilation. After her own Armageddon, Elizabeth had forgotten all about their news, but her quietness went unnoticed for Charles was as happy as a king.

Evers showed no surprise when called upon to bring champagne, Mrs. Frenshaw having apprised the upper servants of Lady Hanthorne's interesting condition. He returned with the wine and, after pouring the glasses, said, "Sir, may I be permitted to say that the staff wishes me to extend felicitations to you and her ladyship." Charles thanked him. Evers bowed again and left.

"A toast, a toast, first to my wife, may God bless her!" Charles lifted his glass high. "To my wife, to my love, to my heart—to Lindy!"

Unchecked tears streamed down Elizabeth's face as she drank to her friend. Charles's declaration of love for his wife was what she wanted from Edward. She raised her glass. "To Lindy, a bright star in a dark world!"

"You know, Beth dear, I'd really given up." Charles became serious. "I can say this now. Yes, I'd stopped hoping. And if we didn't have a child, well we do have each other—that's the important thing! I have a younger brother who could've carried on the line. But Lindy, dear heart, she'd let it get her down. Pack of nonsense, I used to tell her. We have each other."

"Not many gentlemen feel as you, Charles."

"Oh, I don't know. If there is love, how can one feel otherwise? She makes my life a joy, Beth, she does! That we shall have a child is a wondrous thing, but not more wonderful than Lindy herself. I am a very fortunate man."

"May my toast be to you both, Charles dear. To you two, and to the love you share!" It was a solemn moment.

Charles suddenly remembered the duke and asked where he was. Elizabeth said that he had to return home, something required his attention.

"Now I understand why you didn't want me with you," Charles teased her. "Wasn't because I would have been a spoke in the wheel at all. Wronged you, my girl, sorely wronged you."

Elizabeth smiled in answer but more tears came. "It's all right, Charles," she lied. "I'm just very happy."

"Here, take this, Beth," he said, giving her his handkerchief. "The same thing Lindy did to me too. Cried most of the time. No need to wet the world, even if you are happy. Take another sip; that will help calm you." He stood peering at her until he was satisfied she was through. Elizabeth felt wretched to be crying about Danforth, especially at this moment.

"Poor dear Charles," she said. "Although if you do have a daughter, all of this will be good training."

Charles looked stricken. "Beth—I hadn't even considered that it might be a girl, but you know, you're right, perfectly right. It could be, couldn't it?" He paced a couple of circuits around the room as he considered it. Elizabeth sat anxiously watching him.

"But, Charles, surely you would love any child of yours and Lindy's?"

"It's not that at all. Do you know what scares me? I'll tell you. Don't think I know enough to be a father of a girl. Never had a sister. They need a lot of care and protection. My Lord! Of course we could have a girl! Happens all the time, doesn't it? Well, what I mean is, someone has to have a girl to marry all the men. I mean your father had a girl—and so did Lindy's—had four of them."

"Charles!" Elizabeth said sternly, "don't balk! Up and over! What dithering nonsense from such an ordinarily sensible man!" She sat glaring at him.

He stared at her for a moment, and then, as all that he had said came back to mind, he gave a whoop of laughter and rushed over to embrace her. "Now that's my Beth! No nonsense. I was a bit bowled over though, but well, I guess we'll manage with whatever we get. Mustn't mind us new fathers-to-be, love. Some things just take a bit longer to get used to."

Charles then decided that Melinda would be up to a celebration after all, and they took their bottles and glasses upstairs. The mother-to-be greeted them complacently; she had known they would come. Further toasts were made amid much laughter and tears. By throwing herself into their happiness, Elizabeth tried to forget, but it was impossible.

Chapter Thirty

Melinda joined them at the breakfast table the next morning, declaring her day's stay in bed had been enough to last her for a lifetime and that she had things to do. They were glad to see her, Fretty having privately told them that, providing Lady Melinda did not overtax herself, there was no reason to keep her in bed. Melinda would see a doctor later, for now she was content with Fretty, who had seen a sister through several accouchements.

She had a long list in her hand and, after pouring a cup of tea, was ready to share it. "Now this must be first," she said, pointing to the item, new clothes. "I do want to get to London before I start to show, and I must have something decent to get me there. Poor Beth has almost nothing. Lady Warmner promised to send me several fashion journals, and a package of *The Lady's Magazine* and *Ackerman's* arrived yesterday. They're so exciting!"

Charles was not sure she was up to it, but Melinda pooh-poohed him. "That nonsense of yesterday was just to give me confidence. I do swear that if I feel the least bit off, I shall rest. Now—on to Beth. She could be in service, wearing the same day after day."

"Lindy, you are *outré*, outrageous—you really are! I haven't been out of half-mourning more than a few weeks. How many dresses do I need?"

"Beth, now that you've alluded to it, I'm glad, for we've always been open with each other; are you interested in Danforth?"

The dark circles under Elizabeth's eyes appeared

even larger. Charles tried to make it easier by jesting, "Dear Beth, are the intentions honorable?"

Elizabeth burst into tears. Charles and Melinda shared a long look as he asked her to please undo his bungling. Melinda began anew. "Dearest, we have been through so much together, and we cannot help but be concerned, especially when I remember that afternoon you arrived, exhausted and upset . . ." She stopped and intently examined her friend. After a startled look at her, Charles also turned to Elizabeth.

"It is too absurd!" Melinda exclaimed, but after another look at Elizabeth, she demanded, "Beth! Look at me! This is nonsense, isn't it? You and the duke . . . Why, however would you have met? Beth, what is going on?"

Elizabeth wiped her eyes. "My friends, my dear friends . . ." She blew her nose. "There is little I can tell except . . ." She blew her nose again. "There is nothing to say—except that, yes, I am in love with Edward and he does not love me."

They both tried to speak at once. Elizabeth put up her hand. "He asked me to marry him. I refused."

Melinda gave an exclamation while Charles let out an oath so pungent that both women turned to him. He quickly begged their pardon. Elizabeth began to giggle and was joined by Melinda. Charles laughed and they relieved some of the strain in their laughter. When they were calmer, Melinda looked at Elizabeth in wonder.

"I cannot believe it. No, I do not doubt your word, love. Well, you must be fair to us, Beth. It is hard to take in at once. It is!"

"Beth, as long as we have gone this far," Charles said, "please do continue. Why did you refuse him, if you love him?"

Elizabeth was like an abandoned child. "I refused him, my dears, because he finds me compatible. He does not love me."

"He finds you compatible?" Melinda could not believe it. "Why, I've never! Two more incompatible persons I've never seen! Really . . ."

Charles thought. One point needed clarification. "Dear Beth, please do answer me carefully. Why do you think he finds you compatible?"

"Charles, I am not making this up out of whole cloth!" Elizabeth protested. "I know because he told me so; that was the word he used: compatible. As if I were eighty-eight and he ninety and we had best be satisfied with that! I *love*, and he thinks of me as someone who would suit!" She started to cry again.

Melinda got up to comfort her as Charles ran things over in his mind. Charles doubted if compatibility had anything to do with it. The duke never had declared for anyone before; it appeared that he was in love but had botched it. The only way they might help was to stay out of the field—and keep Elizabeth from making any rash moves.

Elizabeth appeared calmer so Charles spoke. "This should settle it, my dears. Beth, of course, will come up to town with us. I've yet to see a female whose spirits are not improved by new clothes and your plans for getting new ones made sound very sensible. But, Beth, if you continue to water everything in sight, I fail to see how any gentleman could find you compatible—unless he be a gardener." He smiled affectionately at them.

Melinda agreed and demanded that he order the carriage for that morning. Elizabeth demured, but was overruled. *No importa*. She might as well be swept along by these dear friends until she knew what she would do. No matter how bleak it seemed at the moment, life did continue.

Life did indeed go on. Melinda kept Elizabeth occupied with trips into Canterbury and Ashford. Fretty's niece came to the house and the dressmaker was consulted. Melinda would not listen to any of Elizabeth's objections, and this time a traveling gown, five day dresses, a town walking dress, a ball gown, and even a lovely cape; all were ordered.

Elizabeth had protested once, but Melinda said she was mulish. "You may be thankful that you are coming back when the fashion is for simplicity and not for yards and yards of fabric and bows and all that. So expensive, and wouldn't suit you either."

"Please don't misunderstand me, Lindy. I seem to have more frocks than I can use for several years ahead."

"Hogwash, Beth! What have you ever known about really being in the thick of things? You came out of your Hampshire chalk downs and rushed up to London to marry Ian and then dashed off to Spain where we tried, but we certainly weren't up to the mode, and then you burrowed down in Margate. Now, and do be honest, have you ever spent any time in London?"

"We spent several weeks there, Lindy. My wardrobe was up to it—not to the height of fashion, I will admit, but I did not shame Ian."

"Oh, and when did Ian ever look at your clothes? His eyes were for you."

"It is true neither of us cared about those things; we were just happy to be with each other." Elizabeth sighed. "Lindy, do you know that I can talk about Ian now? And it is not because he is not still precious to me."

"Yes, both of us have noticed and we're glad. You

won't ever forget the happiness you two had, but it is more than time you rejoin the rest of us in the world. I know I'm repeating myself, dear, but sometimes you are a trifle dense." Melinda grinned at her. She had been careful not to mention the reason for her friend's newfound interest in life. The ever-enlarging circles under Elizabeth's eyes also said there was no further word.

To change the subject, Melinda began to enumerate all of the accessories that must be bought before going up to town. "And gloves, and oh, Beth, we must have some smashing hats. Do you remember that little purple one in *Ackerman's Repository?* There is a little old émigré woman in Canterbury who is said to be absolutely marvelous with her hands. We must try her. Then when we are dressed well enough, we may go shopping in London for clothes." They both laughed at the ridiculousness of it all.

Chapter Thirty-one

The following Tuesday afternoon Mrs. Hubert
Creighdon paid an afternoon call on Lady Hanthorne,
the ladies being at home because of a minor problem with the left rear coach wheel. Elizabeth was
too low-spirited to be able to tell her she was no
longer interested in the "poor neglected men" and
even agreed to accompany that worthy lady to Canterbury on Tuesday next to inspect one of the homes
for old and disabled soldiers.

Elizabeth's hopes that the duke might still join
them as originally planned were dashed when Mrs.
Creighdon said that, although the dear Duke of Danforth could not come with them, he had graciously
given her the use of his property in Canterbury to
do with as she wished.

"I was afraid, for all that I had heard, that I would
find a libertine only concerned with his own pleasure;
however, and I shall so inform my dear friend and
his aunt, the Countess of Richmount, that he could
not have been more correct nor could his sentiments
have been better expressed in this matter. No, I have
hitherto wronged the duke, as I shall be more than
happy to inform all of my friends and acquaintances.

"Why he has not married, I cannot guess, but I
shall consult with the countess, and we shall rectify
the lamentable situation. I shall be more than happy
to introduce him to some worthy candidates. A strong
woman, of noble character, and naturally of good
lineage and fortune, will be an invaluable asset for
him. It is more than time he is setting up his nursery."

She thanked her hostess for the excellent tea and

turned to Elizabeth. "Mrs. Campbell, again I must reiterate how glad I am to be able to guide you in the exercise of your proper duty. As a widow of modest portion who is no longer young and in the marriage mart, you should be dedicating yourself to others less fortunate. A most sensible decision, and one that I shall be pleased to help you put into effect. I shall be at the door at one sharp. Punctuality is a necessary accompaniment in those that I instruct." With a nod to Elizabeth and a correct bow to Melinda, Mrs. Creighdon left.

After the door closed, the ladies sank thankfully back into their seats. What a patronizing, meddlesome woman, but before Elizabeth could explode, Melinda spoke.

"I can shop all day and have innumerable fittings without the need for the tiniest bit of rest, but one hour with *that* woman and I am in pieces. She is so, so purposeful, Beth, that I cannot bear too much of it! I'm off to lie down and be soothed by Fretty. Why don't you lie down too? Oh, dearest, how are you going to endure an afternoon with her?" Melinda kissed her friend and went upstairs.

Left alone with no one to calm or soothe her, Elizabeth thought bitter thoughts against all mankind. It was not fair of her, for Charles and Melinda were good friends, but again she was reminded of how alone she was. The prospects of the life ahead of her—filled with good works and Mrs. Hubert Creighdon—chilled her. But, she reminded herself, she had made her choice.

Charles returned before dinner and said that he had run into Lord Warmner, who sent his regards to both ladies. Warmner had heard through Stephen Dawson that the duke had left for town on Sunday or Monday. Charles did not think it likely, for he himself had seen Eversley at the Boar's Tooth the day before yesterday and the duke was still at Swatow Hall. Charles did not add that the reason Eversley was at the inn was in pursuit of a pretty little barmaid who worked there in the evenings. He did pass along his lordship's regrets at having called three times and finding the ladies out. Melinda expressed her regrets too, but privately Elizabeth was glad to have missed him.

Elizabeth was trying to accept the fact that she might never see the duke again. It had been well over a week since their ride, and there had been no word. If he could avoid her here where they were neighbors, how much easier to do so in London. She was not certain in which circle the Hanthornes would move, but she did remember they all were to be at the same party in less than a fortnight. She thought it sad that he, who found her compatible, would not care to be friends with her. A man such as he was not worth one tear.

Chapter Thirty-two

Charles and Melinda had gone to dinner at the Warmners and the Hamlyns, for although Melinda was occupied with preparations for their transfer to London, she did not care to miss anything. Elizabeth had stayed at home, pleading a severe headache once and a possible ankle sprain the other time. She had tripped over a loose brick as she was leaving the dressmaker's, as much the fault of her new shoes with the higher heel as it was the state of repair of the pavement. Melinda accepted both excuses, but sent Fretty in with cold cloths and more balm tea for the headache. For the foot, a small glazed footbath was discovered in the attic and carried to her room, where Fretty filled it with a mixture of oak bark, wormwood, shave grass, and water. Whether it was effective or whether the ankle was not bruised badly, no one could say, but Elizabeth was able to walk normally the next day.

Thursday afternoon Charles returned from Canterbury with the information that they were entertaining that evening. Melinda gave a wail, then demanded to know more. Elizabeth hoped that Charles was quizzing them. The ladies had been looking at several of the fashion magazines, for Melinda was not happy with the reticules they had selected. She knew what was adequate for Kent, but she wanted to be all the crack in London. Magazines and tea things were strewn around the green room and Melissa had her shoes off. Why tonight of all nights would dear Charles invite someone?

"It is not someone, love, it is a friend—one of

your favorites, too." Charles was enjoying the suspense.

Elizabeth could not help her heart; it stopped for a moment as she waited to know whom. Melinda looked speculatively at her husband, the same thought in her mind. Charles shook his head.

"My ladies, have you only one friend, or two? Do you not remember old friends? Are your affections so fickle that—"

Melinda could tolerate no more. "Charles! If you do not tell me this instant!"

Charles laughed. "Would you not be happy to see John Thompson again?" he asked.

The ladies' expressions of wonder and delight were what he had wished to hear. When they quieted for a moment, he continued, "I ran into him in Canterbury just walking down the street. His mother lives in Deal, if you will remember. He is home on a short leave, for there are some things that he has to take care of pertaining to his father's estate. I told him you both would be happy to see him tonight."

"How could we not be happy, Charles!" Melinda replied. "The only problem is that I think we're having braised ox cheek with stewed cabbage tonight, and that would not be fit to serve a guest." She begged their pardon but she had to consult with cook, and she left.

Charles turned to Elizabeth. "He and Ian were very close. He told me he was very happy to know that you were with us. His limp is gone and he seems completely recovered."

Captain Thompson had been wounded in the same assault in which Major Campbell had been killed. He was an excellent leader of men, and a good friend. For a time it was feared he would lose his leg, then later that he would not ride again, so it was excellent news to know that he was well. Charles, Ian, and John had been an inseparable threesome, and Elizabeth was happy that he would be with them tonight.

Melinda had been correct about the ox cheek, and she and cook spent an anxious hour looking through the larder and consulting with such other and several books. They finally settled on scallops of mutton with oysters (oysters being plentiful and on hand), pork cutlets broiled with a plain sauce and black pudding, salmon cutlets, à la maintenon, baked eels (as cook said, it was not a favorite of Mrs. Campbell's, but she did not have to take any, for there must be two fish. Melinda agreed), chickens à la Toscano, and an omelette. The two soups which already were planned for the evening would do— one being clear, the other a brown one; but the beef dish took much thought. Neither were particularly happy with their choice, but they could think of no other: braised roll of beef, garnished with glazed roots. Two or three vegetable dishes were chosen and, as the guest would be a gentleman, cook would double up on the desserts, the men always liking an adequate selection in front of them. There was a pigeon pie that was going to be saved for breakfast, as was the salmon, but tonight's need was greater.

Fretty was glad there was something else for Mrs. Beth to think about. She herself never had the time to be married, the "Mrs." in front of her name being honorific, but she loved the children of her married sister as if they were her own, and her affection and concern for her lady made her fierce if there were questions about Lady Melinda's happiness. Mrs. Beth came under her protection too, and she was not pleased with his Grace's treatment of her. Fretty's mother, who had been well learned in folk remedies, would have prescribed some marjoram for luck in love; Fretty would put her faith in a gentleman such as Captain John as being the better tonic.

Fretty came in to dress Elizabeth's hair and to be sure that all was well. A deep green wool with a low décolletage looked fine on her; a pity she did not have more jewels, but wishing didn't help and Fretty went to get a rich chocolate-colored shawl from Lady Melinda's drawer to make the frock complete. The hair went all up this time, intertwining strands with each other until Elizabeth looked like a duchess at the very least. Fretty checked her reticule. Elizabeth looked a very fashionably turned out lady.

"Now remember it is Captain John, whom you know, not a stranger. Don't twist the strings on the bag and you'll be all right." She nodded to Elizabeth that it was time to go downstairs.

At first Elizabeth felt constrained, but he was the same John Thompson she had known. A few more lines creased his brows, and there was a suggestion of early gray in his dark brown hair, but he still was a handsome man with ready laughter. He, Ian, and Charles were almost of the same height, tall, commanding men. In his green coat with the military air, he looked the soldier that he was. Elizabeth had valued him for his openness, his lack of airs, and he had not changed.

Everyone wanted to talk at once, for there were so many questions to ask and stories to hear that the green room was too small for their noise. Dr. Murphy was the same, drinking his two bottles a day and prescribing his purgatives for every ailment. "Legs" Humphries had a bullet through his wrist, but it was healing without complications. John had his best horse, Thunder, shot out from under him on the plains, but he had bought another from Dr. Murphy, a strong bay that he liked. He planned to look for another one or two while he was back in England and he and Charles talked horses for a while.

Melinda brought them back to general interests by asking if he had bought some Spanish lace and shawls for his mother. He had, and as he was very well versed in feminine matters, Melinda described some of their new frocks to him and received his approval. He already had told the ladies that they looked like diamonds of the first water.

Then Melinda wanted to know if he were still after Vanderloek's daughter and would not listen when he disclaimed knowledge of the young lady. She prodded him until he admitted his previous interest, but said the lady in question had preferred an Irish peer to a plain English captain, thus allowing the ladies to sympathize with him.

"Now, she was one of your Beauties, John, an Accredited one too, but there was no heart to go with her face," Charles commented. "Do you remember when she sent you off to find the certain flowers, I don't remember which, but she would accept only that kind for her gown, and it took you two whole days to find them. Then that evening she wore Gordon's after all?"

"That is true," Elizabeth said, "but there was another side of her that you gentlemen rarely saw. She was the one who rescued that mangy-looking yellow dog which one of our teamsters was going to kill. She took it back and had it washed and fed, and, while it never was a handsome animal, it was a playful one."

"I don't want to spoil the story, dear Beth," John drawled," but the only reason she rescued it was to spite Dugan, who was wearing his white pantaloons that day instead of his leather breeches, because he wanted to make a good impression on her. She knew how much he hated to get dirty and that he loathed dogs."

"John, that is not kind!" Elizabeth protested.

"Not kind, it's true," Charles supported Captain Thompson, "but I heard the story from Dugan myself, and he is not an untruthful man."

"It was because there were so few ladies there," Melinda said, "and her head became turned with all of the attention. She did not arrive so spoiled."

Charles wanted to know the progress of the war, and although they had talked about it in Canterbury when they met, there was much to discuss. Dinner was announced before they had covered all of the commanders, the change in direction of the war, and of Wellington's new support from London.

Elizabeth went in with Charles, while John brought in Melinda. Dinner was served in the large dining room, the table having been made small so that they did not have to shout. Charles inspected carefully each dish passed to him with such intentness that they all noticed. At last Melinda asked what he was doing and an unabashed Charles admitted he was looking for the ox cheeks to see what manner of disguise they had settled on.

"Lindy, dear friend," John said after their laughter was gone, "I'd happily have humble pie with my friends, and you know it."

"What do you mean you would, John. You have had it with us, and several times when things were short!" Melinda corrected him.

Melinda wanted to know if they were as interested in the Princess Charlotte in the Peninsula as they were at home. The papers said she was at the Splendid Fete which her father, the Prince Regent, had given at Carlton House in honor of the good Queen's birthday. She had danced with her uncle, the Duke of Clarence. John said that they were loyal subjects and naturally the men and officers were interested in the Heir, especially now with the Prince of Orange's name being mentioned with hers.

Colonel McMahon's name was mentioned and, as John had had several run-ins with the paymaster, he was very willing to share them with the others. That they tried to make the rogue keeper of the privy purse and private secretary to the Prince Regent did nothing for Prinny's reputation, but at least it took his hands out of the widows' pension money.

Melinda suggested they talk of happier things, and Charles brought up the Poet Laureate. His wife protested that Pye was not yet dead and it was of other things, lighter topics, that they should discuss, but Elizabeth and John were willing to speculate on the possible candidates.

"They cannot pick another of less repute than the present," Elizabeth said. "Did you ever read *The Progress of Refinement?*"

"If it's anything like *Faringdon Hill*, thank you, no," John replied.

"I suppose Scott would be in the running. The ladies enjoy him," Charles said sourly.

"Why not Southey, he can write," John said. "I don't see how anyone could consider Wharton, although my mother likes him."

Melinda was restless with the literary subject. "How is your younger brother William?" she asked. "Wasn't he to go into holy orders?"

"That is supposed to be the plan, Lindy, but as his latest was to take part in a fair including the goose riding, when he should have been at the books, I do not know what will happen."

"Goose riding?" Elizabeth questioned. "I've never heard of that. What is it?"

"I'm not surprised you know nothing of it, Beth; it is not a sport that ladies care for. It's popular in the rural areas and at the local fairs. A live bird is hung up by its feet with its head and neck well greased. The sport is to pull off the goose's head while riding past it."

"Good Lord!"

"Ugh. Terrible!"

"The matter of William becomes more complicated, for he borrowed the horse from the butcher, without that worthy's consent, and to make it do more than amble, a considerable amount of force was needed." John sat for a moment thinking of his younger brother.

"I once was in my father's black books for borrowing the horse of the tinker who came through twice a year. My brother, Clarence, and I liked the sound of the pots and pans hitting each other, and we determined to see what the sound would be if we really got the horses going." Charles smiled.

"And—what was the sound?" Elizabeth asked.

"I'm afraid we never heard it; however, there was another loud noise, so Clarence, who collected interesting sounds, was happy. The bottom fell out of the wagon."

"I've never heard that story before," Melinda said, laughing.

"There are many stories best kept private, my love."

"Did your brother collect sounds?" Elizabeth wanted to know.

"Oh, yes. He had a book and he entered each sound with all of the appropriate data—what time it was, where it occurred, the reaction to said sound.

He also tried to write out an appreciation of the sound. I found the book once and read it after I was supposed to be in bed asleep, and I woke up the whole floor with my laughter. His descriptions were—well, they were amusing to me."

"What other sounds did he catch?" John asked.

"There were the obvious ones: another brother snoring; the woodpile falling down when our terrier went in after a rat; and our nurse stumbling over the footstool and dropping the tray full of dishes. But there were some really exciting ones too. We had a large black bull, and he did not like one of the stable hands. The lad used to tease him, and one day when it was very hot and no one had very good tempers anyway, he came through the stable wall after the young man. I was fortunate to be crossing the yard to the stables at the time and was next to a fence, through which I jumped. Clarence was with me, and until I shouted to him, he stood there with his ears thrust forward, the better to capture all of the sounds."

"My dears, if you could see Clarence now! He is a staid gentleman, very much the family man with a small estate in Wessex. He is on all of the church committees and patron of this and that."

"But, Lindy, we do not always act in what others perceive to be our character. Each of us have secret parts, dreams, memories that we share very rarely." John smiled at her and turned to Elizabeth for support. "Don't you agree, Beth?"

Elizabeth well remembered her sojourn in the North, a very important secret. "Heavens yes, John. I do agree."

Dinner was over but the gentlemen asked the ladies to stay with them. "I can't imagine what we could say that could top Clarence's noises," John said.

Brandy was served as was port, and all felt the good feeling one has among old friends.

Charles reminisced about a foraging party he had led. There had been no activity for some time, and Charles needed something to do, so he had taken fifty-odd men out into the country. There should be no problem; the orders were unequivocal: no pillage or any disorder, and the mayor of the town was to be paid in Spanish dollars. Some of the villages had wanted nothing to do with them, for they'd suffered under the Spanish army. There had been numerous instances of robbing the villagers of pigs and poultry, even linens. Wives and daughters had been mistreated —all by their own people. The French permitted no license, and soldiers were hanged or flogged for stealing.

They had haggled over two pigs from a certain villager and reached an agreed price, but when one of the men, a trooper by the name of Shanks, had gone to drive them out, he'd been attacked by the small brown cur who was trying to protect his master's property. The dog was small, but the teeth were sharp and he'd caught the man in the calf, just above his boot, and held on. There was so much hilarity over where the dog had him that no one could help, until the old man's wife had waddled out and told the dog to stop.

"That's not a funny story, Charles," said Melinda, cross with her husband. "The poor man could have been hurt. If that is the kind of story you tell when you gentlemen are alone . . ."

"Lindy, dear, the man who was called Shanks was bitten on the calf of the leg," John explained. Melinda looked blankly at him. "Calf—shanks, it's all the same part." Everyone laughed as she protested that it wasn't funny.

"For if you have to explain something that much, it loses its humor," was her pronouncement.

"Surely you know 'shank's mare'? It means to walk, it's an old term." John turned to Charles. "How did he get his name?"

"I would not risk it again," Charles said, smiling at his wife.

"I think that is about the same as the natives here." They looked puzzled. "You know what I mean, you all do. That it is dependent on whether you are born west or east of the Medway. Those west are 'Kentish men' while the others are 'Men of Kent.' Well, what I mean is, it is as funny as your poor man."

Melinda joined in the laughter.

"So you're going to join the dandy set, Charles," John said.

"Not likely, man. No, I'll take my seat in the Lords and manage the property and—" Charles could not think further at the moment.

"And drive through the park and join the clubs and in a while forget that you were ever a soldier?"

"No, I could not, John. Everyone has to have something to do or they get into trouble. Learned that with my men. Same holds true for ladies and gentlemen."

"I want to tour the country," Melinda said. "I've never seen Scotland, for instance."

"That isn't England, dear," Elizabeth reminded her.

"I do know that, even if I didn't say it. I'd like to take the *Comet,* the new ferry that Mr. Bell built last year."

"That's the steamship, isn't it?" John asked.

"Yes, and trust Lindy to want to get on it once before it blows up!" Charles teased.

John could not stay late, for he was riding back to his mother's. They asked him to stay, but he said there were things he had to do early in the morning in Deal. He had only a moment to speak to Elizabeth alone.

"What are your plans, Beth?" asked John. "We haven't talked about you at all."

"If you'd asked me even two weeks ago, I could have given you a statement but now . . ." She shrugged her shoulders. "I'm to go with them to London for a while, and then I guess that I shall find my own cause, a hospital or whatever and become busy."

"I'll be back in six months, Beth. I'd like to keep in touch." John's voice was serious. There was no time to say more, for Charles and Melinda came up to them. John's horse was ready; it was time for him to leave.

In bed that night Elizabeth lay thinking. John was a friend; that she did not feel the excitement that she felt with Danforth did not mean it was a bad thing. There was affection. Why did she want love too?

Chapter Thirty-three

The next morning Elizabeth felt restless. It was too early for spring; perhaps it was the change of the moon. She smiled at Fretty who'd come in to see how she was. This unsettled mood wasn't something she'd make known; it would be more herb tea or some such concoction.

Melinda and she had planned to go to Ashford that morning, but Melinda needed to sleep in, so the trip was postponed until the afternoon. Fretty sensed her disquiet and said she'd do Mrs. Beth's hair—if she sat still.

"I'll tell you a story, Mrs. Beth. Keep your mind off other things, it will." Elizabeth sat down at the dressing table, and Fretty started to brush her hair. "My people come from near Waltham Abbey and we've always been in service, my grandmother being a housemaid, as was my mother. We have Mop Fairs there—Statty Fairs they're called some places—and once a year everyone comes to be hired again or get a new place or start out.

"The men wear clean white smocks and they wear something in their hats to tell what kind of work they do. A waggoner would have a whip cord braided and fixed nicely around his hat. A cowman would have some cow's hair; a shepherd would have wool, and so on. Now the women the same, it was a hiring fair for indoors and out, and the domestic staff would have different aprons. Cooks would have colored ones, nursery maids white linen ones, and chambermaids lawn or cambric.

"There'd be a parade of sorts and they'd all walk around and the various employers would walk around and everyone would look over the other and finally they'd talk and be offered the year's hire. With that out of the way, they'd go to the Punch and Judy show; there'd be an exhibition of a giant, a dwarf, a red American Indian chief, sometimes a cannibal— who knows what they'd have? There'd be throwing for prizes, wrestling matches, chasing a greased pig. Oh, there was something for everybody with loads to eat and drink.

"My grandmother's best friend was a pretty girl of some twenty and eight or nine. She'd been betrothed to an undergardener but he died from the smallpox and she was left alone. She'd saved her money and herself; they were going to buy a small inn when they retired.

"The Squire's son was a handsome enough man, if you like dark men. There were those in the village that thought him a wonder to behold and others, older and more settled, who said he could be the devil himself. He wasn't married, didn't do anything except be the gentleman, but he had children enough to work a farm, if he wanted to turn them to.

"Well, he was at the Mop Fair that year, strutting around not saying a word, just looking over the female servants—and even some of the farm women— and he saw my grandmother's friend, Margaret was her name, Maggie they called her. He started to talk to her. She didn't pay him any attention; she'd helped one of the cook's girls through a bad time with a baby from him, and she knew what he meant. He was piqued because she stood him off; she didn't fall under his spell right away. Not that it wasn't flattering to her to be singled out by him, but she didn't plan on being his next, no she didn't, and she went home earlier than she'd planned as she didn't want to be tempted.

"That went on for a few months with word going around the country that he'd found a harder nut to crack this time. They started making bets in the inns about how much longer she'd hold out, for he'd never lost one yet. My grandmother spoke to her, but what can you say to someone who's that way? Maggie said it wasn't anything but a ring on her finger that she'd accept.

"And who's to deny he was a charming man. He was rich, handsome, and he knew the words to the female heart. He should, he'd unlocked enough of them in his time. Oh, no, it was the talk of the county.

"Well, for the first time in a long shot, you've set still, Mrs. Beth." And she showed Elizabeth the results in the mirror, and made ready to leave the room.

"Fretty," Elizabeth called, "why are you leaving? What happened?"

Mrs. Frenshaw made an unexpected smile. "Why, Mrs. Beth, what did you think—he married her, he did, and when his father died, Maggie became the Squire's lady," and she continued out of the room.

The day was unremarkable. The Ashford trip took up the afternoon; and both ladies felt the same unease. Melinda said it was because they were ready for town and should be going up. Elizabeth felt that had something to do with it but that John's visit yesterday had brought back many memories.

"John is interested in you, Beth. I'm sure he is," Melinda said, watching her friend.

"John likes me, he does not love me. Do I need

212

yet another that views me in that manner?" Elizabeth asked wistfully.

"No, Beth. Is a man who disputes with you all of the time more interesting than someone like John? A brave, sensible man? And he is entertaining too—if you'll remember."

"Lindy, do not plan my wedding! Yesterday was the first time in almost two years that I've been with the Captain. Instead let us talk of things that we may truly count on—your babe-to-be, for example."

Melinda knew she was being diverted from a subject, but when it was to one close to her heart she did not mind. Charles and she would discuss Elizabeth later. Now she would talk with Beth about her baby.

Chapter Thirty-four

After dinner on Saturday evening a hired coach stopped in front of Swatow Hall and a young man dressed in a creased uniform of a subaltern of the —Nth got out. He held up his hand and helped a young girl in a rumpled ball gown descend. He continued to hold her hand as they went up the steps, pressing it tightly and smiling down at her, before he took the knocker. The noise frightened his companion, and she looked up at him for reassurance. He bent to give her a kiss on the forehead before he rapped on the door again.

It took almost five minutes before the door was opened. Dodson stood looking at them. The visitor cleared his throat, stood erect, and said in a very loud voice, "Announce me to the Duke of Danforth. I am Mr. Arthur Westnett and bride."

Dodson was unimpressed. It was late and his master was not entertaining these days. "I am sorry, sir, but his Grace has left orders not to be disturbed." He started to shut the door.

"But I must see him! I am his cousin—Lord Frawling's son. He'll see me."

Dodson frowned. It did change the nature of the call. The Honorable Arthur Westnett was family; but on the other hand the duke did not care to see anyone.

"And besides, the coach has been paid off. We've come all the way from London just to see the duke!"

Dodson peered out and to be sure, the taillights of a coach were disappearing down the drive. Two small bags sat on the gravel at the foot of the steps, and as he brought his gaze back, the young couple were looking expectantly at him.

"Well, sir, I am afraid that I do not know what to do," Dodson admitted. "You may come in while I consult with Mr. Parker." He opened the door wider as they entered. Their coats were removed and given to a footman who was standing in the hall. "I suppose you had best wait in the morning room. This way, please," Dodson said as he started down the hall.

Lord Eversley was on the landing of the stairs, peering down. "Dodson!" he called. "Thought I heard a devilish racket awhile back." Little enough was going on these days that he wanted to miss anything.

"My lord, these are cousins of his Grace," Dodson explained.

"Then just a minute and I'm down," and his lordship hurried down the stairs.

"Arthur Westnett, at your service, sir. My wife, Mrs. Westnett." The young man bowed while his wife made a small curtsy.

"Eversley here. Call me that or Richard. My pleasure." He bowed to Mrs. Westnett and stretched out his hand to her husband. "Rum time of night to pay a call though, Westnett. Rum time."

"Sir, I was trying to advise them of that," Dodson said. "His Grace was emphatic that he was not to be disturbed."

Eversley regarded Dodson thoughtfully. "Oh, has he? Well, don't expect me to do the dirty work."

"Sir!" Dodson took it to heart that his lordship would suggest such a thing. "I had thought of consulting with Mr. Parker."

"Capital, man, capital idea!" Eversley said, clapping Dodson on the back. "That's just the thing. Good man. I'll take them with me down to the morning room and if you'll just pop back with a bottle, we'll be all set until you and Parker get this straightened out." He motioned the couple to follow him.

Such familiarity would be unforgivable, if it were anyone but his lordship. His kind disposition had made him a favorite in the household, especially now that the duke was in a difficult temper. Dodson himself went down to the cellar to find a very good bottle for Lord Eversley.

In the morning room the young couple too were falling under Eversley's spell. It was not long before they began to regard him as a friend and to want to confide in him.

"You see, sir, it has not been that easy for us," the Honorable Arthur began. "We were just married this morning."

"No, you don't say!" Lord Eversley pumped the young groom's hand again, and bending over the pretty little bride, he kissed her hand. "My best wishes, that's the thing!" He went back to an earlier question. "Still can't understand coming here though. Wouldn't be where I'd go on my wedding night—not that there's anything wrong with bringing her here, but . . ." He shrugged his shoulders at the groom.

"My good sir, that was not my intention at all!" Arthur protested.

"Oh, sir, this was farthest from our thoughts. Indeed it was," his wife agreed.

Dodson entered with a small tray containing several bottles and glasses. "I was not sure what madam would wish so I took the liberty of including a light sweet wine, sir."

Eversley waved him over to the round table. "That's

all right, Dodson, but better go back and get some champagne as well. It's their wedding night."

Dodson was circumspect. "How nice, sir. My congratulations, Mr. Westnett. My best wishes, madam." What a ravelly tale for Mr. Parker—what a tale.

After they each had a glass and had received Lord Eversley's toast for their lifelong happiness, his lordship seated them again and waited for their story.

Mr. Westnett began. "It is my mother and my wife's mother that are the problem, for both of our fathers would be agreeable, if their wives would let them. Even my commanding officer stood up with us; if it had been as havey-cavey as my mother says, he would not have had anything to do with it."

"Artie," his wife broke in, "do let me explain, for although what you say is true, it might be better to start at the beginning." Her husband agreed. "It would be easier if I told you what were the plans made for us. Made by our parents—or rather our mothers, for both of our fathers want what will be best for us.

"Sir, my mother has always wanted me to marry someone of consequence and when Mr. Godwin's wife died, Momma was sad for herself, for she had lost a valued friend, but she was also happy because that left Mr. Godwin a widower, a widower of forty-three, and fat, with three terrible children." Her husband made a motion as if to check her, and she quickly said, "I know you say that I should be as kind as possible, but I am also trying to be truthful, and they *are* grossly spoiled, unmanageable creatures!" She nodded vehemently.

"Mr. Godwin's property adjoins ours, so even Papa could see that it would be a *good thing* if our property could be joined. The only problem was, although I was the oldest, I was only sixteen. Momma said we should not worry, for he must go through black gloves for a year and by that time I would be seventeen and even though I cried and cried, I would become accustomed to it." She looked into the fire for a moment and sighed.

"But you see, I never did. So Momma allowed me to go to some of the parties and balls in the neighborhood, though I was so young, so that I would have some amusement before I was shut away with Mr. Godwin."

Lord Eversley had listened with growing outrage. "But surely, my dear Mrs. Westnett, in this modern age—"

Her husband who had been pacing the room, returned now to stand by her chair. "I am afraid, sir, that my wife is not exaggerating the situation. Her mother, unfortunately, has always been deficient in those tender sentiments which we always associate with motherhood." Lord Eversley regarded him warily.

"Colonel Cardwich, our commanding officer, took a group of us up to hunt, and as I have a good seat, I was invited to join the party. He also arranged to have us included in some of the festivities, and thus we met." He put his hand on his wife's shoulder and smiled down at her.

She returned his smile, and to his lordship's relief, resumed the narration. "I know that it didn't mean as much to Artie as it did to me, for he is used to London and the real balls there. Oh, but for me, it was heavenly to dance and talk and—it was such fun!"

"Oh no, Ceel," her husband protested, "I truly did enjoy it. While I have been through the London seasons, the girls all are so rigid. They must be afraid of making a mistake, for to do so would be to receive a setdown, or worse, a reprimand from their mothers.

To be with you, dear Ceel, was to enjoy them for the first time."

"Well, we did meet," she continued, "and Momma extended an invitation to Artie and to several of the others to call, and there were supper parties and teas and all sorts of glorious things—until Momma discovered that Artie was only a younger son and had no hope of being anything but an 'honorable' all his life. She then told me I might not receive him any more, nor stand up with him for any of the dances, but I would not cut him as she wished; my heart was engaged."

"As was mine, dearest wife," the Honorable Arthur responded fondly. He went over to his lordship, the better to explain. "Sir, we could talk without constraint, for we were not shy in each other's company. It was very soon that my own heart was caught. Then, when she told me she could not see me again, it was as if the light of my days had suddenly been extinguished, for I knew that I loved her. Still, I would not have said a word, but when she further explained she was to marry her neighbor in five month's time, I had to speak and declare for her then and there!"

Mrs. Westnett was blushing. "It was fortunate that I had elected to tell Artie of the necessary change in our relationship whilst we were very much alone—I am afraid that I was most improper, for we had slipped into a small room far away from the others—because I fell into his arms when he told me that he loved me and I was happier than I ever had been in my life! I would not have wanted anyone to have been a witness to that."

Dodson returned with a bottle of champagne in a silver bucket and an additional bottle on the silver tray. He opened it and served them. After Dodson had been dismissed, Lord Eversley again proposed a toast to the newly united pair, wishing them years of happiness together. They thanked him for his kind wishes and exchanged loving smiles with each other. Then Mrs. Westnett put down her glass and became very serious.

"It was a most dreadful time for us, and Momma said that I was looking pale and it would not do, as she elected to take me to a healthful place where I would recover my animation and the color in my cheeks. Papa booked rooms for us at Margate, for its air is highly spoken of.

"My father has a distant cousin who, or so Momma always said, threw everything up for the love of a soldier and ran off with him, and then he was killed. Momma discovered that the sad woman who walked the pier twice a day was this same cousin, and she felt it was a good moral lesson to me to see how everything had turned out for Cousin Elizabeth—but it did not make me feel that way at all. It gave me my answer; I too could run away! I even spoke to her, asking if she was Elizabeth Campbell, for if she were, I admired her, but we had no time to talk.

"We returned home. Momma was in good spirits because I looked so well. It was not the air, but my answer, and I had hope!"

Lord Eversley was staring at her, and had been since the mention of Elizabeth Campbell. He was too polite to interrupt, but as Mrs. Westnett had paused, he quickly asked her to repeat the name. When she did, he could no longer keep the amazement to himself. "Madam, I have the honor of being acquainted with Mrs. Campbell." They stared. "Fact of the matter is, she's staying near here," and he smiled proudly.

Cecelia jumped from her chair the better to hear. "Cousin Elizabeth—and you know her?" He nodded happily. "Artie, is it not wonderful? For you see, if the duke will not help us, perhaps she will."

Lord Eversley was brought back to the present by the duke's name. "But what I don't understand is why are you here to see Danforth?"

"I was coming to that," the bride answered, going back to her chair.

"My light, I fear we are bothering Lord Eversley with all of the details of our sad plight," her husband admonished.

"Not a bit," Eversley answered untruthfully. "Don't say it. Just can't figure out why you're here—wedding night and all."

"I shall enlighten you, sir," and the Honorable Arthur took up the story. "It was Ceel's idea to elope. Not that it had not occurred to me as an answer to our dilemma, but I could not in all good faith ask such a gently reared girl to do something so contrary to her upbringing."

"And what nonsense, dear husband," Cecelia interposed, then turned to explain to his lordship. "It was the only way that we could be united and at last I convinced him of that fact. Who knew when he might be off to war—and Mr. Godwin was getting ready for gray. I escaped from the house, taking all of my pin money, and traveled to London by stage, where Artie met me." She held her head high.

"What courage, Mrs. Westnett," Eversley said admiringly. "What pluck."

"His commanding officer and his wife stood up with us, and then Artie took me to meet his mother." She frowned. "At least, I don't have to be so embarrassed for mine anymore, for his mother was not . . . was not very civil."

"Wasn't civil at all," her husband confessed. "I am

sorry to be forced to admit it. Would not even receive Ceel. Wouldn't listen to me." He inspected his dirty boots. "My father tried to remonstrate with her, but there was no taking.

"I'm not thick in the pocket, sir," he said, squarely facing the older man. "But it never has mattered to me. I have a small yearly sum from my grandfather's estate, and I can count on a bit from my father, but I'll never be able to hobnob with the Hyde Park set —nor have I ever cared to."

"I neither, my dear," his bride affirmed.

"I always wanted to go into the army and my father was able to get me in. My mother, on the other hand, wanted me well set up and kept introducing me to young ladies with fortunes. Now, any girl with blunt that has to look at a younger son with no prospects— well, sir, you do know what sort of female she would be."

"By George, do I!" agreed his lordship. "Could tell you a tale or two—course, not at the moment. Ah well . . . You mean to say that when your mother found the knot'd been tied, she kicked up a row?"

"Exactly! She refused to meet Cecelia, and in fact, told me that she wanted nothing more to do with me! I did not know what to do. I could not take my wife to my bachelor digs, and then I thought of cousin Edward. He is the head of our family and has been kind to me once or twice in the past. I thought that if I could but explain all to him, he might consent to talk to mother. She does kowtow to him, you know."

"Most people do," Eversley agreed.

"But when we arrived at the duke's residence," Cecelia said, "we were told he was in the country, and we did not know what else to do but come here."

She became very grave. "For if I must be sacrificed, let it be to a man of my own choosing, and we shall

222

be happy for as long as God gives us. And this is something I do not understand. If I am old enough to be married, why cannot I make some decisions in matters pertaining to me? When I asked Momma, she told me to be quiet and that she hadn't finished my education yet, but that she was sure Mr. Godwin could be depended upon to continue it, for I was just a green girl." She tried to keep them back, but a few tears escaped from her eyes.

Her husband took her hands. "My dearest Cecelia, please remember that all of this is past. I *am* your husband." He lowered his voice and whispered comforting things to his bride as Lord Eversley set across from them, trying to pretend he was not there.

Chapter Thirty-five

Dodson had gone to consult with Mr. Parker, who was not sanguine about the young couple's prospects of an interview with his Grace but promised to see what he could do. Nothing could be fairer, and Dodson waited in his wife's sitting room with a glass of port while the valet went to the library.

Parker's pessimism was well founded, for although the duke was only into the first bottle of brandy, his mood was foul. It was not easy during the day to keep his mind away from Elizabeth, but keeping engaged in various activities helped. He found it hard to understand; his pain seemed as fresh as if she had rejected him ten minutes before. She wanted him as a friend; he wanted her as a wife. Danforth wanted no company in the evenings, not even that of Lord Eversley, who had taken to nightly visits into Ashford. The only person that the duke wanted to be with was the woman who had refused him. He knew his behavior was that of a fool, but he didn't know what else to do and so, each evening, he brooded alone in the library.

Into the middle of these dark thoughts Parker intruded. The duke paid him no attention, but his valet was used to his master's ways and was willing to outwait him. This the duke also knew, but he took his time before he looked up and growled, "Well?"

"Sir, you have company."

"I also have a butler, Parker. He is paid to refuse admittance to everyone."

"Yes, sir. These visitors are your family."

"The devil take them all, Parker! I suppose Dodson was too blue-livered to tell me this?"

"Yes, sir. They are Mr. Arthur Westnett and bride."

"And bride." The duke echoed the valet's words, then laughed harshly. "He's not dry enough behind the ears to be married yet. Not that his unspeakably maneuvering mother hasn't been parading wool-merchant's daughters and the like in front of him for several seasons." In spite of himself, his curiosity was aroused. "What's she like?"

"Nothing of that sort, nor a touch of the shop, Dodson felt. A 'quiet pretty little thing' was his description."

"Well, I'm not here to give a blessing on young lovers." And he laughed at the thought. "Tell them to get back to town."

"Unfortunately, sir, they arrived in a hired coach which has departed already."

"Oh, has it?" He thought for a moment. "Well, put them up for the night and then send them packing. I'll be damned if I'll see them—and be sure they understand it."

"Yes, sir," Parker said, and he left to carry the message.

Dodson thanked the valet profusely. "I am greatly indebted to you, Mr. Parker. I did not dare intrude on his Grace. Your courage is to be marveled at, it truly is. Now I shall inform the young gentleman of his Grace's answer. Not that it was unexpected, but mark my words, Mr. Parker, there is more to their story than we know. Do you think the duke might relent in the morning and see them?"

Parker refused to hazard a guess and went to his room to wait until he was called to help his master to bed.

Dodson delivered the news to the morning room. He was sorry that the answer was thus, especially as little Mrs. Westnett took it so hard. But in spite of her tears she thought of another solution.

"It will have to be Cousin Elizabeth," she said firmly, but then as she thought longer, she became despairing again. "Although what she might do, I have not one idea. Perhaps there is no one who can help."

"Now, now, Mrs. Westnett, chin up. Mrs. Campbell has her wits about her. Handsome woman too." Lord Eversley was trying to think of reassuring things. "Send a message to her, first thing in the morning. There, that's the ticket!" He turned to Dodson, who was still waiting for instructions. "Dodson, we need a note sent to Mrs. Campbell at Greenfields. First thing in the morning."

"Yes, sir."

"She's cousin to Mrs. Westnett here," Eversley explained.

"To be sure, my lord."

Dodson went for writing materials and Lord Eversley tried to compose a note in his head, explaining all in just a few sentences, for he was damned if he'd go through the whole story with all of the "ifs" and "buts" and "howevers" the way he'd received it. There must be a way to shorten it, and he worried it over in his mind.

Dodson returned, but Eversley still had not hit on the exact way of telling Elizabeth the whole story in three sentences. After "My dear Elizabeth," he bogged down. Cecelia offered to write the note herslf. Eversley was happy to accept her offer, but warned, "No book, mind you. Keep it short. Tell her the rest when she gets here." His inspiration had arrived! "That's the

thing. Just say you are here and she's to come too."
He smiled. "Friend of the duke too."

Cecelia could not reconcile her impression of poor
Cousin Elizabeth with a woman who, as his lordship
assured her, was a good friend of his and the duke.
"Are you certain that your Mrs. Campbell is my cousin?" she asked timidly.

"Oh, absolutely. Duke even knew her husband, the
soldier. Told me so himself. She's staying with the
Hanthornes, old friends. No, no doubt of it."

Dodson wanted to be helpful too. "Mrs. Campbell
paid the duke a visit almost two weeks ago."

This time it was Lord Eversley who was surprised.
"Eh—Dodson, what's this? First time I've heard of it."

"Well, sir, the visit was for his Grace. A commision
for Mrs. Hubert Creighdon, I believe."

"Oh that." Eversley was relieved to understand it.
"Still is odd neither mentioned it to me."

Cecelia gave up her effort to understand the trans-
formation from poor gentlewoman to a friend of
members of the *ton* and went to the task of composing
a short letter. The final missive wasn't as short as Eversley would have wished nor as long as Cecelia
would've liked, but it did say they hoped she would
call the next morning for they needed her help. It was
put into an envelope, and sealed, and given to Dodson with the charge from his lordship that it be delivered the first thing next morning.

"Oh yes, sir, and if that will be all, I can show you
to your bedroom when you are ready," he said to the
Westnetts. And then, because Mrs. Westnett was such
a young thing, he added, "And perhaps his Grace will
reconsider in the morning and will receive you."

"Do you think he might?" Mr. Westnett asked.

"Shouldn't get our hopes up, Westnett," Eversley

answered. "I doubt it. Ain't seeing anyone. And look at the bright side—just as well not see him. Foul mood."

In a short while the bride and groom followed Dodson to their bedroom for their wedding night.

Chapter Thirty-six

The note from Swatow Hall arrived before Elizabeth was awake, both Lord Eversley and Parker having stressed to Dodson that it was imperative she receive it early. The footman who carried it to Greenfields impressed this fact on the footman who received it, and who in turn presented it to Evers. By this time an aura of life and death surrounded the note, and Evers felt it best to consult with his master.

Charles had risen early and was in the breakfast room having his second cup of tea. After he heard Evers's explanation, he examined the note but could not recognize the handwriting. He had first thought it was from Danforth, but the hand clearly was that of a schoolgirl. How a young child was in the duke's household and would be writing to Elizabeth, he failed to understand. The most sensible thing would be to send it up to Elizabeth and see what it was all about. As it was evidently of great importance, he would accompany her to the duke's. It might also be time for those at the side to step in to give the principals a hand.

He told Evers to send the note up to Mrs. Frenshaw, who could give it to Elizabeth. She also should be told that the carriage would be ready in half an hour and he would be with her.

Evers personally gave the note to Mrs. Frenshaw so that he might tell her of the mystery and urgency surrounding it, as well as deliver his lordship's own message of the carriage and his company. Mrs. Frenshaw only gave a "humph" to all of Evers's words and went to deliver it to Elizabeth. Once inside the bedroom door, however, she stopped to examine it again and think it over. The handwriting stopped her, she had to admit, but if things were starting to move again, well more power to them. Almost anything would be better than this unhappy in-between state. This settled, she awakened Elizabeth.

As Elizabeth had not been able to fall asleep until the early morning, she was not easy to awaken. Fretty had to shake her shoulder and call her name several times before she answered.

"There is a note for you, Mrs. Beth. Best sit up and read it," Fretty said.

Elizabeth was not quite awake, but she sat up and took the envelope, trying to look at it. But her eyes were not ready to be used, and she could not even make out her own name.

"One of the duke's footmen brought it 'round first think," Fretty said. There was a look of such hope on Elizabeth's face that Fretty quickly added, "No, it is not from him."

Elizabeth looked up to Fretty, her eyes becoming awake now.

"No need to look at me that way." Fretty smiled at her. "Read the daft thing. That's always the best way. Then you'll know what it's all about."

Elizabeth broke open the seal and opened the letter. "Fretty! It is from my Cousin Cecelia! She is here, but the duke will not receive them—them?" She looked to Fretty to make some sense of it. Fretty took the letter from her hands.

"Well, firstly, she don't write with a very well-formed hand." Elizabeth shook her head, and Fretty continued. " 'Twould make it easier to decipher if we could read it. Yes, it would!" She too shook her head.

"She stayed, or is staying, for the night at the duke's?"

"I think so, Mrs. Beth, or else his mother's, for I'm certain that I can make out the word 'mother' here."

"For heaven's sake, Fretty, his mother is dead!"

"Well, somebody's mother's around. No, the only thing clear is blank-pray-blank-come-to-blank-blank as possible. Blank-blank smudge, help, and then she's signed it 'Cousin Cecelia.' How old is she?"

"Sixteen or seventeen."

"The hand is more of an eight-year-old, I'd say. But for something you can understand: his lordship also sends a message. He'll be waiting for you in twenty or so minutes and will take you to Swatow Hall in the carriage."

Elizabeth leaped out of bed and then reached for the robe which had fallen to the floor. "I can't understand what she is doing at his place. Are you sure it came from his residence?" Fretty nodded. "He does not know her. I do not understand it." She had one of her day dresses in her hand when Fretty stopped her.

"You'll want to be dressed better than that over there, Mrs. Beth. He hasn't seen the dark brown long-sleeved one. Off with the nightgown first, please."

As she dressed, she tried to think what might have happened to Cecelia. Could there have been a carriage accident? But if she were eloping, this was not the route to Gretna Green. . . . She looked horrified at Fretty. "He has not married her!"

Fretty told her to hark. "Two things, Mrs. Beth. There are those that work well while they talk and those that talk better than they work, and if you want to be ready when his lordship is, you had best be quiet for a bit. Not only that, but I can't see as how you've been able to get any bit ahead for all of your figuring things out. You'll be able to find out everything when you get there, so let me get you ready to go."

Elizabeth sat down to have her hair done. "I'll do

it simply, never fear. Up it will go on your head. I think I'll get Lady Melinda's badger fur hat. That and the muff that goes with it will be just the thing."

Fretty went off to get the hat and muff and returned with them and Melinda's deep-brown cashmere mantle. One hook had to be fastened in the middle of Elizabeth's back and after redoing it, Fretty looked her over. The frock's high stand-up collar fitted perfectly around her neck; the skirt fell straight, the hem was even. With the round badger fur hat perched just off to one side, a little of her blond hair showed, a very nice contrast. With the muff and mantle, she'd be turned out to a hair.

Charles was waiting in the hall as Elizabeth and Fretty came downstairs. He put away his pocket watch and wished her good morning. "Good soldier's training again, you're right on the dot. How pretty you are this morning, my dear." He gave her a kiss as she greeted him. "How your heart is pounding, Beth. *Tranquilizate*—it won't be long before we're there."

Elizabeth wanted no food, so Fretty gave Evers the mantle and he helped Elizabeth into it. The carriage was waiting. There was a light film of snow on the ground, and Charles insisted on wrapping another robe over Elizabeth.

After they'd become settled and the carriage off, Charles asked, "Well now, Beth dear, what's this all about?"

She shook her head. "Charles, I can't make head or tails out of it. It is my Cousin Cecelia and she is at Edward's. Why or what or anything, I have no idea."

"But the note, my dear?"

"To be useful, Charles, you must be able to read something. I cannot—neither can Fretty. Cecelia asks for my help. Beyond that I know nothing."

"Then would you prefer to sit quietly and worry or shall we talk on something?"

She laughed in spite of her strain. "Charles, you dolt, I don't care!"

"It will either be about the rebuilding of the Drury Lane Theatre, about which I know nothing, or the Luddites, and I will be your schoolmaster."

"Why the Luddites? Charles, your many facets continue to amaze me!"

"Because I can't think of anything further from your mind than that." He leaned back and began, "We haven't been troubled, overmuch, here in Kent, but in the North their rioting's been extensive. Last month's hanging of the fourteen in York was to prevent expansion of the movement as well as to punish." He continued to talk, and in spite of herself Elizabeth found herself becoming concerned about the problems of the workingmen in the industrial centers of the country. She had not known the extent to which the high unemployment and low wages had made the workers fear mechanization.

The subject only lost its power to hold when the swaying of the carriage told them they must be turning into the drive.

Elizabeth was grateful. "Thank you very much, dear friend."

"Not at all, Beth. Don't forget I'll be taking my seat in the Lords soon. Our country is changing, even if we do not generally notice. Ah, here we are." He smiled at her as the carriage stopped.

Chapter Thirty-seven

Dodson had not bothered to tell Parker about the bride's relationship to Mrs. Campbell until the following morning. Parker was extremely annoyed; Dodson protested he had not thought it important or he would have come to Mr. Parker . . .

The valet made himself be calm. "Mr. Dodson," he said quietly, "any mention of Mrs. Campbell is of the utmost interest."

Dodson could not believe him. "But, Mr. Parker, Mrs. Campbell—"

While Parker knew his master's feelings were engaged, he had not had time to discover whether hers were too. Now would be an excellent opportunity to do so. He had lived through almost two miserable weeks with his Grace and was determined to bring this matter to a successful conclusion. How he was to do so, he did not know, but he would even enlist the services of Dodson, and it seemed that he must impart certain information to him.

"Mr. Dodson, his Grace holds Mrs. Campbell in the highest esteem."

Dodson sat down, awed both by the news and that Mr. Parker would share it with him. He thanked and rethanked the valet, vowing that he would do anything Mr. Parker wished. "Anything, no matter how small, that I hear regarding Mrs. Campbell, I shall immediately inform you."

Parker acknowledged his loyalty and went to wake up his master. The note had left for Greenfields at daylight so it was imperative to get his Grace to receive the Honorable Arthur.

But the duke had already decided he would see the young man. Even if he were in the glooms, he could help in someone else's happiness. "Give you odds, it's his mother that's pulled the rug out from under him," was his first remark to Parker.

"Sir?"

"Sophia—the Countess of Frawling. You remember her. Had her on my neck a couple of years ago when she was trying to get Youngers to come up to scratch for her second daughter."

Parker too clearly remembered the Eriny. His Grace had given her an excellent dressing down at the time. "She is the mother of the groom?"

"Unfortunately, yes. She was a Yettering; never liked that blood. Married my cousin Robert, a decent enough man. Wants his peace and to live in the country; she likes the social life so they live in London. She's married off three daughters and two other sons, and in between she worked on Arthur. His father consulted with me when they were considering the army. I told her at the time to hold the reins loosely on the boy. What's the problem this time?"

Parker made no answer but went to the windows to draw open the curtains.

"Now, man, you can't tell me you don't have an inkling," Danforth prodded.

"No, sir, I have not spoken with him. I do know, however, that they were married only yesterday."

"Aha!" the duke chortled. "I was right! So it was Special License and run to his Grace to make it right with Mother!" He got out of bed and went over to look out of the window.

"So I'm the lesser evil to face. That's doing it up brown. Still I can understand why he bolted, should have years ago. Bit of snow, Parker." He became pensive. "I think I've had enough of the country life."

Parker, correctly surmising that his master's thoughts were on his lady, felt it best to bring them around to the young man's problem. "You will see him, sir?"

The duke turned back to the room and began to dress. "Yes, but not until I've some food in me. There are some things that should never be brought up until the belly is full and I suspect this is one of them. And I'll only see him; can't stand tears. How much Sophia wanted an heiress. Almost feel sorry for her—son running away with a bride from where? All of the Mrs. Grundys will be out."

"This jacket, sir?" Parker asked as he held up the black double-breasted.

"Yes, that's fine. How old's the girl?"

"About seventeen, Dodson thought."

"Damned young, Parker, too young. Arthur must be four or five years her senior. I've never found them attractive that young." He began to tie his neckcloth.

Both master and man waited until the folds were perfectly creased. "Not bad, Parker." The duke stood for a moment looking at his reflection in the mirror. "I feel old. It is more than time to stop this running. Well, Parker, what would you say to a trip to Italy? We haven't been there for a while."

"Whatever you wish, sir. I shall be happy to accompany you."

"Faithful man, Parker."

"I count it an honor to be able to serve you, sir."

This caught Danforth's sense of humor. "All of the time, Parker? I can remember a few instances when it appeared you were not approving." He laughed. "And some of the ladies that you did not find up to standard."

"Very true, sir," Parker answered, "but that was some time ago." The two men inspected each other thoughtfully.

The duke looked away first and he turned to pick up the folded handkerchief which Parker had laid out for him. When he turned back to tell Parker he was ready, his face was expressionless, but his eyes were those of a wounded man. Parker lowered his eyes and held the door open for his master.

"Tell Arthur to come to the library at ten. I'll see him then."

"Very well, sir." Parker closed the door. *En vérité*, his master was more than ready to settle down! Now to meet Mrs. Campbell and judge her feelings. The very proper Parker smiled as he thought of himself playing the role of cupid to such a pair—but a pair that he wholeheartedly could serve. First he must work out this slight impasse.

All went smoothly according to Parker's design. The duke breakfasted below, the newlyweds received a tray in their chamber, and Lord Eversley was still sleeping. Parker wanted to separate the husband and wife so that each would be interviewed by their champion without knowledge of the other. That could be done, and as for his lordship—he was free to wander in and out as he chose, but for the moment, Parker could not think how it could be prevented.

Parker sent a message in to the Honorable Arthur requesting an interview. When he appeared, Parker was pleased to see him dressed and asked if he could immediately come to the library, for the duke would see him after all. There being no time to advise his wife, Mr. Westnett was shown into the library and told it would be only a few moments before his Grace would come. Parker also advised the young man not to mention the note sent to Mrs. Campbell. It would only muddy the waters. Then he went back upstairs to remind Mrs. Westnett of her cousin's imminent arrival. The bride was seated in the morning room before the duke left his table. All was ready.

Chapter Thirty-eight

Dodson opened the door, greeting Elizabeth and Charles as if they were old and valued friends of the family. Elizabeth made some reply and, seeing Parker coming down the hall, went to question him. Parker gave her a warm welcome; he was happy to see her and to note the dark circles underneath her eyes. He smiled reassuringly but denied any real information other than her cousin was eagerly awaiting her in the morning room.

Charles was impressed at the welcome afforded Elizabeth. It was clear, the upper servants were in the know; that the duke's man would seek her out, treating her with the most proper deference, meant that he entirely approved. How this was to help in the real test when Danforth and Elizabeth met, Charles couldn't guess, but he was glad he had come.

Elizabeth asked to be taken to her cousin and Dodson took Charles and herself to the morning room, the small parlor where Lady Langley used to sit. It was a cozier room than most in the house with blue, white, and yellow chintz curtains, comfortable chairs, and two old blue Chinese carpets. Pictures of ships interspersed those of dogs on the walls.

Cecelia had been pacing the room, trying to collect her wits. She stopped when the elegantly dressed woman entered. Although she was greeted as "Cousin Cecelia," she couldn't answer. Here was no drab, sad-eyed widow but a handsome woman of the first water. Cecelia was very conscious that she was wearing her second-best ball gown, those the only dresses she had packed when she made ready to leave her home. She had been married in one, and this she had been wearing when Artie proposed. She wished she'd brought some day frocks too.

Lord Hanthorne was presented to her, but again she could do no more than curtsy. Charles smiled. "My dears, if you will forgive me, I shall retire to the far corner and look at several of the books I see on the table. If you need me, however, I am here." He left them to talk.

Elizabeth took her cousin by the hand and led her over to a sofa. "Come, we shall sit here, and you may tell me all about it." After they were seated, she asked, "Did you not receive my note?"

Cecelia nodded. "Oh, yes, ma'am."

Parker entered and asked that Lord Hanthorne excuse him, but he would deeply appreciate a few moments of his time. Charles nodded. "Sir, I believe you to have Mrs. Campbell's interests at heart." The two men looked at each other, trying to read the other's mind.

Finally Charles answered. "That is correct."

"And, sir, I am concerned with the duke."

"To be sure," Charles agreed.

"I wonder, sir, if you might accompany me into the hall where we might discuss this further?"

Charles didn't answer but rose and, with a nod at the two women on the sofa, followed Parker out of the room.

"Lord Eversley has awakened and is partaking of his food in the breakfast room," said Parker.

"You don't want him popping around, is that it?"

"Just so, sir."

"And I'm to keep him occupied and out of the morning room?" Parker nodded, and Charles continued. "Well, only for a trade, man. Where's your master and what goes here?"

"His Grace is in the library where the young lady's husband has his ear."

"You're playing a deep game—but for God's sake, don't tell me about it. Take me to Eversley and I'll keep him out of the way."

Happy to be readily understood, Parker bowed and showed Charles to the breakfast room.

Back in the morning room Elizabeth was trying to make sense of Cecelia's disjointed recital of her elopement. "But, my dear girl," Elizabeth exclaimed, "can you not understand—I did not run away! And you said you received the note I left at the White Horse. Didn't you read it at all?"

"Oh yes, Cousin Elizabeth, I received it. Thank you so very much. It showed me how I might communicate with Artie through notes left at the inn."

Elizabeth was indignant. "Good God, girl—how could you! I just aided you in your love affair!"

"That isn't fair," Cecelia objected. "You yourself said that your father loved you and wanted you to marry your Ian. I wasn't so fortunate! My father does love me, and he's told me he is sorry it has to be this way, but he could not protect me or help me in any manner."

Elizabeth calmed down. "All right. What is done is done. But you know they will say you've made your bed and will have to lie in it."

A blush crept over the bride's face and she lowered her head. Elizabeth laughed. "Perhaps it's not so bad after all. Your Artie does have some sense, I trust? You seem to be the one who has led him astray."

"Oh, do not say that!" Cecelia flared up. "Artie is the best, most loving, kindest, nicest gentleman in the whole world!"

"We shall have to hope so," Elizabeth answered dryly. "Now we must decide what can be done. You want the duke to intercede for you with his family, but you surely are not counting on me to do the same for yours. I do not even know your mother."

"I wouldn't ask you to do that, ma'am." Cecelia tried to think exactly what it was she wanted Elizabeth to do.

In the library Arthur was trying to condense his story yet cover each relevant point, only becoming entangled occasionally. The duke listened boredly until Cecelia's encounter with her cousin in Margate, and then he became keenly interested in each particular, even making poor Arthur backtrack several times to fill in details. Arthur had not dared hope for a kind reception, and he became more confident, finishing his story without much trouble.

"And now you have come to me to fish you out of this trouble and make your bride acceptable to your family," said the duke, for you are fond of them even if your mother, at times, goes beyond bounds. And as for your bride, you want me to explain to her family why you are so much more acceptable to them than the worthy Mr. Godwin. That is all, I presume. You are in good stead with your commanding officer, so I need not concern myself there."

"Oh yes, sir," his cousin replied, very relieved that his older relative so easily understood the problem.

Dodson entered to announce, "Mrs. Campbell to see you, sir."

Elizabeth stood in the doorway. "If I might have a word with you—alone." She walked into the room.

Danforth had instantly risen at her entrance. He bowed, noting how well her dress became her and that there were large, black circles under her eyes.

Elizabeth would not quite look at him but went

over to the young man. "You must be Artie. I am Elizabeth Campbell." She held out her hand.

He too had risen and now he tried to shake her hand, bow, and stammer greetings to her.

"Come now," she said kindly, "I understand we are cousins."

He looked up into her blue eyes. "Yes, ma'am."

"From all that Cecelia has told me, she's led you a merry pace. I hope that you can keep up with her."

"Madam—cousin, you do her wrong! Ever the gentle lady, she has always been—always!"

Elizabeth and Danforth laughed, and Elizabeth glanced at the duke; their eyes met, ending the laughter. Both saw the strain in the other but did not know what to do. Oblivious to their absorption, Arthur was trying to correct their impression of his bride; his words droned on as they inspected each other, then there was silence.

The duke found he had kept Elizabeth standing and smiled apologetically. "My dear, I am sorry. Do sit down. My manners seem to be shot."

Elizabeth demurred that she would not be that long. The door opened and a flustered Dodson entered. Danforth glared, ready to throw him out.

"Sir, madam, do forgive me, for I know you are . . ." Dodson faltered for a moment, then carried on. "Lord and Lady Frawling have arrived."

"Good Lord!" Arthur regained his voice first.

The duke was contrite. "My dear, you are about to meet my cousin, Sophia. I am sorry to say that there is nothing in your family to equal that!"

Elizabeth was shaken, yet game. "Sir, you have not yet met Cecelia's mother."

"Elizabeth, my dear, you are not proposing to make a wager?"

She smiled. "Never fear, it would be stealing, sir." She walked to him and touched his arm. "Edward, I do need to talk to you. They need your help."

"And you're asking me?"

She met his eyes. "Yes, I am. I am asking as a friend."

His voice was cold, his eyes stern. "I am aware of that too well, my dear."

"Please don't look at me that way. You cannot hate me so."

"Hate you! It matters, Elizabeth?" He caught her shoulder before she could turn.

The door was wrenched open and a tall busily dressed woman strode in. "I don't care what he is doing, I am entering. He must be made to realize that the family honor is at stake!" She had spoken to someone behind her. The door was shut and she stood arrogantly waiting for their attention.

"Mother!" Arthur squeaked.

"Damnation" was the duke's comment as he let Elizabeth go. "Well, Sophia, I suppose that manners have nothing to do when honor is at stake?"

She was moving toward her son, but stopped. "Edward, I am so glad that you recognize what I mean." She turned back to her third-born. "And you, Arthur. I presume you have been filling Danforth's head with all sorts of nonsense while we were home, worrying the whole night?"

"Do sit down, Sophia." The duke indicated a chair. "This is all very wearing. I thought my cousin Robert accompanied you."

She chose a straight banister back chair and sat down. "Of course, Robert is here. Where else did you think he would be with his middle son in such an entanglement? He preferred to wait in the hall until we were allowed entrance. I, on the other hand, told your butler that I would not stand on ceremony and I entered."

"So I see."

The door opened and Dodson ushered Lord Frawling in. The earl was a few years older than his lady and, while her whole bearing was one of purpose and determination, his was of care and misfortune. His face was unhappy as he made his greetings to the duke and tried to apologize for barging in.

"Nonsense, Robert," his wife said sharply. "What Edward has to do that is more important than our matter, I would not know!"

Lord Frawling tried an apologetic glance at the duke, receiving a small smile in return.

"Elizabeth, may I make my cousins, Lord and Lady Frawling, known to you? Mrs. Campbell." The duke remained at Elizabeth's side.

"Charmed," the earl said, bowing, while his lady gave a slight nod. Elizabeth nodded and smiled at them both.

"My parents, Cousin Elizabeth," Arthur explained.

"Cousin!" Lady Frawling shrieked. "You cannot be related to that—"

"Be careful, Sophia," the duke warned.

"—to that Jezebel that trapped my child? Oh, sharper than a serpent's tooth is an ungrateful son!" She glared at Elizabeth and Arthur, but as they were on opposite sides of her, she was forced to constantly turn to do so.

"In order to avoid a spasm, Sophia, I would calm yourself," Danforth kindly advised. "Dodson, do bring a tray of something and ask Mrs. Westnett if she would join us. We might as well have a proper family party."

"A family party! Edward, how can you jest at a time like this?" Lady Frawley's displeasure was great.

"She seduced him, that is what she did! The marriage shall be annulled."

Before Arthur could complain, the duke answered her. "The marriage was consumated here under my roof, Sophia. I think you forget that your son is over age. If any parent could protest seduction, I am afraid it would be hers." The countess became livid.

"Edward," Elizabeth said softly. "I should not be here."

"Of course you should, my dear," he answered equally quietly. "We shall get you into the family this way, if you will not choose the other."

Elizabeth went white. "That was uncalled for, Edward, and you know it!" Her chin jutted up; she was furious.

Danforth was now a relaxed man, completely in control, for he was sure that Elizabeth cared for him. Her reactions were not of a lady embarrassed by an inopportune lover, but rather of one who cared deeply. Why she had refused him, he did not know, but he would take care she did not again. He must take note never to propose on horseback, and almost laughed aloud, for he planned on only doing it once more in his life. He smiled, caressing her with his newly discovered happiness, until Lady Frawling, who had been upbraiding her son, turned to him and complained.

"We shall be the laughingstock of the whole town!"

"Then the answer is simple, Sophia," Danforth answered. "Retire to the country for a while. It will soon blow over."

For the first time since he entered, Lord Frawling's expression lightened. "I say, Edward, that's a damned good idea. Sophia, did you hear him? I think that's a good idea."

"Oh, don't be a fool, Robert!" she snapped.

The door opened and Cecelia entered. Dodson had felt it only fair to warn her that her new mother and father were present, and, although she had wanted a meeting with them since yesterday, she was thoroughly terrified. Arthur rose at her entrance and went over to her, an act which made him stand higher in everyone's eyes—except those of his mother.

"I suppose you are going to tell me, Edward," began Sophia, "that I had best swallow this insult to my pride, cast all my hopes asunder, and—"

"Yes, dear Sophia, I am. There will be little remark when it is known that she is welcomed into the family. Their wedding night with the head of the family . . . It doesn't sound that bad, does it?"

Elizabeth went over to the countess. "Those who dare to say anything, Lady Frawling, can be told that while you deplored the rashness of their conduct, it was a very romantic thing to have done. And if there is a smile whilst you speak of that romance, they too will soon be caught up in that tender sentiment. And," Elizabeth added, "your voice, I am sure, will add weight to Danforth's statements."

Lady Frawling had started to bridle when Elizabeth began, but the more she listened, the more sense she discovered—particularly in the last sentence. The duke was proud of his Elizabeth's adroitness and in an aside told her so. He added further words in support of Elizabeth's suggestion, and Lady Frawling began to look upon him kindly.

Dodson came in carrying a tray filled with bottles, followed by a footman with the glasses; they went to the large intarsia table and set them down. At a nod from his master Dodson opened a bottle of champagne and began pouring. As Lady Frawling was talking with Elizabeth, the duke went over to the earl.

"It wasn't my idea to come here, Edward," Lord Frawling hastened to explain.

"Spare me, Robert. I am only too well aware of that. It may not be the match you planned for Arthur, but it's the marriage he now has."

"Know it, Edward, know it. Seems a nice enough little thing." They watched as Elizabeth went to the young couple and brought Cecelia to her new mother, Arthur following protectively.

"Madam, your daughter, my cousin Cecelia." Cecelia did not dare look up at that stern face but made a deep curtsy. "I know that you will want to give them your blessings after they have prettily begged your pardon," said Elizabeth. "They should not have frightened you so."

Lady Frawling was going to say something else, but instead she followed Elizabeth's lead. "There was no need to have been married in such an underhanded way! I was so worried!"

Cecelia's upturned face was appealing. "Ma'am, please do forgive me. Artie is the most wonderful, kindest person that I have ever known. I should not wish to be on the outs with *his* mother."

"Let no one say that I was hardhearted, child. I had to have the best interests of my son above all else."

"She won't bring you great wealth, but she loves your son and will honor you," Elizabeth added.

"The blood's good, Sophia," the duke said, "and when Arthur is ready, I'll buy him his captaincy as a wedding present." Taking a glass off the tray which Dodson was holding, Danforth presented Lady Frawling with a glass of champagne.

That lady knew when to accept defeat, especially when she was being helped to do it gracefully. She gave the duke a small smile and looked at the couple in front of her. "Well, it seems as if it has been taken out of my hands. You may kiss me," she said, giving her cheek first to Cecelia and then to Arthur. "Just promise me faithfully that you will never do it again!"

Danforth and Elizabeth laughed.

"I'd like to know what I've said that was so funny," Lady Frawling asked.

"Happiness, my dear Sophia, that is all. May I, as head of the family," and he included the whole group, "propose a toast to the newly wedded couple." Everyone looked at the lovers and raised their glasses. "To the uniting of lovers." Just before he drank, the duke caught Elizabeth's eyes and held them while he drank to her.

Elizabeth was confused. His glances were of love, not friendship; but if he loved her, why had he not said so? He was not a backward man.

The earl thanked Danforth. "Darned good of you, Edward, to say you'd buy Arthur his captaincy. Much obliged. Didn't think I could go that high for a while."

"Don't mention it, Robert. I am happy to be of assistance. Now, I have a suggestion. If you could take your family into the drawing room, there is a fire there and Dodson will bring the tray. We shall lunch together and of course you'll stay the night. I know there are many things you'll want to talk over with the new couple. Mrs. Campbell and I have a matter to discuss and then we'll join you."

Lord Frawling was all happiness. For years his Sophia had tried to wangle an invitation out of Danforth but had never made it. He must point out how much they owed to the youngster's marriage, and he went to his wife to relay his news.

Lady Frawling was so conscious of the honor that

it took ten minutes to clear the room. At the last her husband took her by the hand and led her out. Elizabeth and Danforth were left alone.

The duke stood smiling at her. "You are shameless, love. Do you know that? Such buttering up to Cousin Sophia."

"Edward, you were not behind me in that!" Elizabeth was quick to answer. "I must be going. Good heavens! I've just remembered—Charles. I'd forgotten all about him! He came with me; what on earth could have happened to him?"

He ignored her question and came over to her, took the glass out of her hand, and put it down. "Elizabeth, my love, look at me," he commanded and he took her hands in his. "I asked you this once before and you said 'no.' I am going to ask you again, but this time the only answer I shall accept is 'yes.'"

Elizabeth did not know what to say. It was important that he understand why she could not accept him—though she loved him. "Edward," she began and her body started to tremble, his hands on hers bringing shocks to her being. "Edward, I know many people manage to do so, but I cannot marry for companionship." She would like to cry but his eyes held hers.

"Elizabeth, you ninny—who said anything about companionship?"

"Who said? Why, you did!" She tried to break free, but he held her hands tighter.

"Some day I shall be able to laugh at this, my love, but not now. Did you really, truly think that the only reason I wanted to marry you was that I liked your company? You cannot be such a dunce, my dearest!" She did not answer. "Answer me, damn it, Elizabeth!"

"I did," she said very softly.

At that the duke let go of her hands and took her in his arms. "Elizabeth, my love, my life, I love you —I *love you!*" He shouted. "I love Elizabeth Campbell, I do!" He pressed her tighter. "And you cannot tell me you do not love me." He reached down, bringing her lips up to him, and all of the happiness in the world was in their kiss.

The door opened; Charles started to enter, saw them embracing and stopped, then decided to come in after all. He shut the door with a bang, and they quickly moved apart.

Edward was facing the door and saw Charles first. Taking Elizabeth by the hand, he led her to their friend. "Charles, be the first to wish us well."

"Edward, you are impossible," Elizabeth protested. "I have not said yes."

Charles smiled broadly at them. "Well, if you haven't yet, my dear, you'd best say so now. Enough of this playing fast and loose." He bent to kiss her.

"Come, my dearest, I think it best before a witness," her lover chided.

Elizabeth's blush spread. "I will have to—to save my reputation, if for no other reason."

"For no other reason?" Edward asked.

There was no other way to stop such an inane conversation, so Elizabeth said, "Yes, Edward, oh, yes."

Love—the way you want it!

Candlelight Romances

Once you've tasted joy and passion,
do you dare dream of

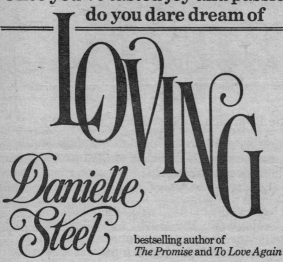

LOVING

Danielle Steel

bestselling author of
The Promise and *To Love Again*

Bettina Daniels lived in a gilded world—pampered, adored, ador-
ing. She had youth, beauty and a glamorous life that circled the
globe—everything her father's love, fame and money could buy.
Suddenly, Justin Daniels was gone. Bettina stood alone before a
mountain of debts and a world of strangers—men who promised
her many things, who tempted her with words of love. But
Bettina had to live her own life, seize her own dreams and take
her own chances. But could she pay the bittersweet price?

A Dell Book ═══════════════════════ $2.75 (14684-4)

INTRODUCING...

The Romance Magazine For The 1980's

Each exciting issue contains a full-length romance novel — the kind of first-love story we all dream about...

PLUS

other wonderful features such as a travelogue to the world's most romantic spots, advice about your romantic problems, a quiz to find the ideal mate for you and much, much more.

ROMANTIQUE: A complete novel of romance, plus a whole world of romantic features.

ROMANTIQUE: Wherever magazines are sold. Or write Romantique Magazine, Dept. C-1, 41 East 42nd Street, New York, N.Y. 10017

INTERNATIONALLY DISTRIBUTED BY DELL DISTRIBUTING, INC.

The first novel in the spectacular new
Heiress series

The English Heiress

Roberta Gellis

Leonie De Conyers—beautiful, aristocratic, she lived in the
shadow of the guillotine, stripped of everything she held
dear. Roger St. Eyre—an English nobleman, he set out to save
Leonie in a world gone mad.

They would be kidnapped, denounced and brutally sepa-
rated. Driven by passion, they would escape France, return
to England, fulfill their glorious destiny and seize a lofty
dream.

A Dell Book $2.50 (12141-8)

Dell BESTSELLERS